THE MARVELL COLLEGE MURDERS

THE MARVELL COLLEGE MURDERS

A   NOVEL   BY

SOPHIE BELFORT

DONALD I. FINE, INC.
NEW YORK

Library of Congress Cataloging-in-Publication Data
Belfort, Sophie.
The Marvell College murders / by Sophie Belfort.
p. cm.
ISBN 1-55611-255-6
I. Title.
PS3552.E474M37   1991
813'.54—dc20   90-56080
CIP

Manufactured in the United States of America

10 9 8 7 6 5 4 3 2 1

Designed by Irving Perkins Associates

The world, my dear, is far from incorruptible.

MONTESQUIEU, *The Persian Letters*

ONE

O N MOST ISSUES, Margaret Donahue knew where and with whom she stood, and rarely in the past had she found herself even close to Marvell College. Now, Marvell's Center for Participatory Politics was offering her a fellowship—an honor, the director of its midcareer program assured her, she had earned many times over by her notable achievements as an urban educator and forceful spokesperson for her invaluable, underappreciated profession. Margaret sensed that her long devotion to public education did not by itself account for this tribute: a newly elected congressman, who told her he couldn't have won without her, had suggested she apply. He'd apparently hit upon a year at Marvell as a form of spoils she might accept, and he'd chosen well, for she was tempted—wary, but mightily tempted.

Marvell College, which lent its luster to the Center for Participatory Politics, took its name from Andrew Marvell, who had procured the school's first government contracts. After long association with the Puritan cause, the poet had been chosen, in 1659, to represent the city of Hull, his birthplace, in Parliament. Almost before he reckoned those tidings could have reached the New World, he received an entreaty from Massachusetts settlers whom he had known at Trinity College, Cambridge. They told him of their struggles to maintain a seminary in the wilderness: the beacon fire they had lit flickered distressingly. Providence, they trusted, would not permit its extinction, but Heaven helped those who helped themselves.

Andrew Marvell quickly secured for his old friends a commission to render into the Algonquin and Iroquois tongues sundry elegies lamenting the death of the Lord Protector, written the previous year. In 1660 Marvell was able to renew the grant, this time for the translation of odes celebrating the accession of Charles II.

In gratitude, the divines renamed their school Marvell College, and to emphasize for the new regime their break with Calvinist iconoclasm, they erected a statue of the poet, looking as if he had world enough and time to grant many favors. Subsequently, lines from Marvell's poem "Bermudas" were carved on the statue's pedestal, though some people feared the inscription would cause future generations to confuse the Deity with the donor.

> He cast (of which we rather boast)
> The Gospel's pearl upon our coast.
> And in these rocks for us did frame
> A temple where to sound his name.

In the next three centuries, the school grew to be a vast university, although, with conscious archaism, it still called itself a college. Altars were paid for and built, in every generation, with the founders' ready eclecticism. The small flame Andrew Marvell stoked became a blazing pyre; rare was the moth that did not fly to it.

"So, Molly, what do you think?" Margaret was meeting in an hour with Emory Stokes, the director of the midcareer program. She had come early to case the place with her friend Molly Rafferty, who had studied at Marvell. "Should I accept the fellowship?"

"Why, apart from Marvell's appalling employment and investment policies, do you hestitate for a moment?" Molly asked.

"And housing," Margaret considered the university a rank slumlord, anachronistic in its shamelessness. "My God, just look at this place. It's obscenely rich." The two women were walking across a brick quadrangle enclosed on three sides by the Center for Participatory Politics.

"Take the fellowship, Margaret. You work hard. This might be fun." Molly Rafferty had gotten her doctorate at Marvell and knew the place as well as she wished to know it; she was determined, nonetheless, not to prejudice her friend. Margaret deserved the recognition and needed the rest. She chaired the art department at Newnham High School—a grim place, Molly thought—supervised art instruction city-wide and ran the local teachers federation; on her own time, she fought to keep the blue-collar city she loved from succumbing to the ugly backlashes that perennially convulsed it. "The Center does attract interesting people."

"It looks as if it's lying in wait for them," Margaret said, though she was neither fanciful nor easily frightened. "Like a sphinx. I don't know whether it's the yellow stone or the copper mirror glass."

"The Center looks a little jaundiced in November, but it's Eldorado in the summer sun."

"No, it's not just the gloomy light. Its proportions are threatening. The main building looms over the wings," Margaret persisted, "like a strange beast crouching to spring."

"The beast faces south, you see," Molly laughed. "It's slouching toward Washington to be confirmed. Let's see some other buildings." She felt sure Margaret would prefer an older, plainer aspect of Marvell: the redbrick schoolhouses of a new and hopeful Republic.

"About Washington," Margaret said, "I don't want to seem ungrateful." She took political debts seriously, paying her own promptly and letting other people discharge theirs. The director of the midcareer program had called her himself to set up this interview, and she was certain he had done so at the urging of the congressman-elect.

"It would please him to help you to a year at Marvell." Molly believed the candidate did owe Margaret Donahue a great deal. The campaign had been frightful, even for Massachusetts, marked by the murder early on of the front-running Democrat. "Is Emory Stokes still the director of the midcareer program?" She did not add that she had known him as "Tremblin' Em," trembling with drink and eagerness to please.

Instead, she emphasized Marvell's stimulating diversity as she led her reluctant friend on a tour of the campus, bringing her back to the Center on the stroke of four, in good time for her meeting with Emory Stokes.

The Center's shallow front steps recalled Margaret's first impression: the beast's lower jaw on which she was standing lolled deceptively slack, ready to snap shut. Maybe it wouldn't like her. Maybe it would spit her out.

A security guard looked up from his newspaper as they entered, incurious but formally vigilant; he checked the day's appointments on his clipboard and waved them down the corridor before bending again over a list of the week's lottery winners.

"I'll wait for you in the library," Molly said. "Come and find me when you're done with Stokes."

"Or when he's done with me." That seemed to her a more likely outcome. "Thanks for coming with me, and staying."

Margaret rejoined her friend, sometime later, subdued and plainly troubled. She had not wanted to be seduced. "I don't care about prestige," she said.

Molly, who had been reading in an oversized armchair upholstered with Marvell's imperial purple, looked up and closed her book. "No one who knows you imagines you do. It went well, then?"

"Stokes dropped more names than any political has-been I've ever met." She herself dropped into another armchair, facing Molly over a table in a small alcove. The library encouraged conversation rather than solitary study.

"You recognize the type. But Stokes isn't Marvell's heaviest hitter. Did he say anything about the other fellows?"

"He claims they've got a top-notch troubleshooter from the UAW and somebody from the Garment Workers, but no one at all from public sector unions." That appeal had moved her.

"An omission they should remedy," Molly agreed. "And, I'll bet, not enough women."

"You're right. Stokes regrets they have so few fellows of what he calls the 'feminine persuasion.' "

"That's a nice touch. 'Feminine persuasion' makes gender sound optional, as if you're free to change your mind."

"You're content with yours, I imagine," Margaret said. Her friend taught history at Scattergood College, a small, selective women's college, and she was living, blissfully to all appearances, with the detective who had solved the campaign's sensational murder shortly before the primary.

"Quite content." Molly did not flaunt her happiness. She was in an early, incredulous stage of love, full of tender pity for species who fertilized their eggs externally, but she knew she was lucky. Sex made lots of people miserable. "In any case, however condescending Stokes may have been—" Molly paused. "Did he actually say 'role model'?"

"Several times."

"He's right, though. There are women on the faculty here, not many, but some. But undergraduates almost never meet women with your practical experience. You'd be an eye-opener. You'd be an inspiration."

"Let's talk about this someplace else." The surroundings were too rich, the appeal too plausible. Margaret wanted to think things over in her dingy office at the high school, at home, anywhere but here.

They walked out through shelves of periodicals; as they approached the tall racks from which airmail editions of the world's major newspapers hung suspended, a bellowing voice shook the thicket of crisp pages. "Where the hell is my *Financial Times?* It's after five o'clock. It's supposed to be on my desk when I get here in the morning." The red-faced man stopped when he saw the librarian and cut short her apology. "Sorry to come chargin' in here, sugar. I didn't know you were working this afternoon. I know it's not your fault. The morning girls should see to it. Don't you worry one little bit."

The librarian, who had risen to meet him, resumed her seat.

"I know that young woman," Margaret said. "She went to Newnham High School."

"She's lovely."

Anger forgotten, the *Times* subscriber bent with boyish eagerness over the librarian's desk. The young woman sat, respectful and impassive, unable to work until he left, but powerless to dismiss him. He spoke at length, ingratiatingly. She answered briefly. He continued, entreating; she shook her head, with its long dark hair. Finally, he patted her hand. "So long then, honey. I won't see you again till I get back. I'll bring you a mirage or something from the desert."

"Who is he?" Margaret asked. Molly told her the man was Bertram Harding. She'd heard of him. He did op-ed pieces and television commentary on a variety of subjects. "He spreads himself a bit thin."

"He has wide-ranging interests," Molly said, with a real effort at self-mastery. "And he does take no for an answer."

"I guess you know that for a fact?"

"Yes."

"Molly, what do you really think about Marvell?"

"I think it's an experience you should have."

*   *   *

WHEN EMORY STOKES received Margaret's letter, he sent her a pot of mammoth bronze chrysanthemums. Her willingness to accept a midcareer fellowship, he said in the note accompanying the flowers, gave great pleasure to everyone associated with the Center for Participatory Politics, and especially to himself. He hoped she would find time to sit as an advisory member on a very important search committee. So few of his colleagues shared her grasp of political reality.

TWO

NORMAN CLAWSEN DROPPED BY the Center's library to make sure his latest book was getting the attention it deserved. Satisfied that the staff had done its best for him, he sought out the prettiest librarian and asked if she'd seen Professor Harding.

"He left last night," she told him.

"Don't you remember, Norm?" Emory Stokes had come into the library to consult an atlas. Aspects of Bertram Harding's announced itinerary were puzzling him, and he wanted to check a few details. "Bert's gone off to see the emir again."

"You would think, wouldn't you," Clawsen said bitterly, "he'd care enough about his own reputation, if not Marvell's, to keep his corrupt body out of the Middle East for a while?"

Stokes shrugged. "Bert'll never change. Say, your new book looks great, really significant."

Clawsen would have liked to tarry, gathering compliments, in the library, but he wasn't a man to rest upon his laurels. He hurried on to his office, where stacks of the new book, *Optimization or Alienation: a Mathematical Model of Voter Self-Imaging and Party Realignment,* awaited him. He did not pause to caress a volume or to page through it, but set to work at once, composing apt, handwritten greetings to accompany each copy he was sending out. His wife had typed the address labels that were clipped to the dust jackets. Clawsen shared a secretary with two colleagues, but he preferred that the others not know for certain where his complimentary copies went. He would mention a few names and keep them guessing about the rest. Professional networks, he knew, were most imposing when obscure, their compass only glimpsed and endlessly conjectured.

He wrote diligently on his own letterhead, and this he did contemplate and handle with pleasure: MARVELL UNIVERSITY, it read, in splendid letters across the top. Beneath that pinnacle, and Clawsen liked to think upholding it, were three lines of smaller type: *The Center for Participatory Politics* at the right margin and *Norman N. Clawsen, Professor of Political and Societal Statistics,* on the left. Clawsen filled the rich, heavy sheets with his minute, beautiful script. "See page 274," he advised the editor of an important journal, "I there utilize your seminal study of off-year, crossover voting in border-state gubernatorial contests." To the chairman of an up and coming political science department in the Southwest, he wrote, "You will note that I acknowledge, both in my introductory preface and in my methodological appendix, your path-breaking work." And he cautioned an acquaintance at Yale, "I hope you have decided not to tenure Greenburg. Chapter Nine refutes his baseless assertions about the salience of religious affiliation in the presidential primaries of 1976 and 1980. He lacks scientific foundation for imputing to other hopefully more rational individuals his own fanatical worldview." To Yale, Clawsen would have preferred writing *Weltanschauung;* he tried several times to spell the word, but the arrangement of its vowels eluded him and someone had walked off with his dictionary. It was too damned easy to get into other people's offices.

Years ago the professor had inscribed every volume he gave away. He ceased to do that after finding, one snowy afternoon, a copy of his second book, completed in the fullness of his joy after being tenured at Marvell, in the cut-rate bin of a used book store—$2.00 for any volume, three for $5.00. He had sent that copy with a heartfelt, perhaps somewhat inflated tribute to a man prominent in the field, a man often called upon to referee articles for scholarly journals or to review grant proposals and whom, as it happened, Clawsen had respected enough to propose as a reviewer for a cherished project of his own. It was impossible to tell if the eminent authority had read the book before discarding it. Its pages were not dog-eared. Nothing had been scribbled, fraternally or argumentatively, in its margins—nary a "how true," not even an NB here or there—nor did it open easily to any particular page. Clawsen, seeing it, had remembered hearing that books printed abroad needed their pages cut with a paper knife. He'd sensed then the utility of this practice. The only marks upon the book, and these grieved him, were stains on its cover: sets of intersecting circles. Glasses filled with ice, he thought, whiskey glasses most likely, had been set down negligently and left until water vapor condensed on their sides and trickled down, defacing, deriding, his scholarship. Clawsen never inscribed books now.

When he finished his letters, he rose and walked to the window. His ground-floor office was not the Center's most sought after. The large walnut desk he insisted on having took up a third of the floor space; five or six paces brought him to the lone window, which looked out onto the parking lot. By this time in November, freezing rain had stripped the last leaves from the poplars that screened the lot, and storm clouds, black as asphalt, were massing again above the enviable and unenviable cars left there by the Center's faculty and staff.

Clawsen acknowledged that this was not a picturesque view, but no one could deny its advantages. He saw who came and went, when they arrived and when they left. Some of his colleagues came in only for their mail, some turned up for meetings. Clawsen spent most of his waking hours in his office. Of all the places he might spend time, it was the most congenial to him.

Everyone in the world who mattered, Clawsen believed, or had recently mattered or would ever matter passed through the Center for Participatory Politics. The Center was more than a think tank. It was a political force. Its glamor was world-class; its influence, uncontested and unfathomable. Powerful and famous people mingled there with professors from Marvell's political science and economics departments and from its School of Law. Clawsen loved the chummy reciprocal deference that exalted both parties: "You should know, Professor. You wrote the book." *"You* should know, Your Honor. We may write the books but you throw them at people."

Very eminent persons, called Distinguished Fellows, came to the Center for brief visits unless they were deposed or lost elections; in that event, they might stay for years. If it became apparent they would never resume power, they were either kept on as Permanent Visiting Fellows or turned out as fellows emeriti. Lower in status than these, but still useful to know, were the midcareer fellows.

Midcareer fellows—bureaucrats, business executives, labor leaders, local office holders, journalists, citizen activists—stayed at the Center for one or two semesters to study more formally and mingle to their mutual advantage with Marvell students. They mastered the jargon and memorized the quips they would use for the rest of their lives to confound less privileged rivals. Corporations, federal agencies and several friendly governments paid top dollar for Marvell's cachet, and the midcareer program could make more money than it did, Clawsen thought, if certain of his colleagues stopped awarding scholarships to lettuce pickers and seedy community organizers.

Clawsen glanced out the window and saw one of those openhanded men, Sam Sternberg, a professor of labor law, not a political scientist or a colleague in any true sense, but a power at the Center nonetheless. It was largely Sternberg's doing that some of those scruffy midcareer fellows were sitting, where they had no place, on an academic search committee. But Sternberg was a great democrat. He used his office to meet with students. He had asked for, Clawsen had heard and not at first believed, a smaller desk: Sternberg wanted room in his office for several armchairs because, so he was reliably reported to have said, he did not like talking with students across a desk. He liked to chat with them face-to-face. Easy to be egalitarian if you or your wife were rich, Clawsen reflected.

Sternberg was kissing his wife and getting out of the driver's seat. She got out too, because the car, an old Peugeot, had bucket seats. She came round to the driver's side and laid her hand on her husband's arm as he turned to go inside. She said a few words in her clear, emphatic voice—Clawsen caught "pony," "vet," "darling," "legal services," "darling" and "chevre"—and leaned forward to kiss him again. Clawsen heard Sternberg laugh and say, "I don't want to start anything I can't finish," as he put her into the car and closed the door. When a marriage conferred advantages such as that one did on a man, Clawsen thought, he has to look as if he's enjoying it.

His own marriage had conferred no advantages, although at the time it had seemed a good idea. Audrey had shared his faith; with touching fervor, she'd believed him innately superior to the fraternity boys and lettermen on that distant Midwestern campus. "You are cut from finer cloth, Norman," her blue eyes seemed to say. "You are destined for greatness." Her pale gaze had fixed upon him. Her eagerness flattered and stirred him, and she had been even more tremulously inexperienced than he was. She had thought it daring to lie in her slip in his arms, and those exploits had pleased him too. Audrey had not been especially pretty or popular, but she did belong to the sorority from which homecoming queens were invariably chosen and she looked essentially like them: blonde, credulous, enthusiastic.

A student knocked on Clawsen's office door. "May I see you for a few minutes this afternoon, sir?" The long-limbed youth wore dirty running shoes, khaki pants and a faded crimson sweatshirt stamped "Groton Crew." Clawsen had reluctantly agreed the previous spring to advise his senior honors thesis; one never knew how well-connected these kids might be, or to what heights their zeal and connections might carry them.

"Not today," Clawsen replied. "I'm immensely busy. I'm chairing the search for the new assistant professorship in American electoral behavior."

"So I heard. It must be a terrific responsibility."

"Yes, it is," Clawsen affirmed, picking up his fountain pen. "I've had very little time for anything else this term."

"I wanted a word with you, briefly, about my thesis. Could I leave an outline and a draft of the introduction for you to glance over?" He took a manila folder from the notebook under his arm. "I've got to go to New York for a few days and I'd like to know if I'm on the right track."

"New York, eh?" Clawsen wondered whether the boy was going down for a debutante party or for interviews with some firm that paid its summer interns more than he made in half a year. "Party?" he asked.

"No, I've got some interviews."

"Wall Street, I suppose?" The boy was a junior Phi Bete, but that and five dollars didn't buy you much Perrier.

"No, sir, I was lucky. Made the first cut for the Rhodes. I don't know if I'll get to the regionals, but everybody says the state interviews are a lot of fun."

"Well, have fun then." Clawsen began to shuffle through

the papers on his desk. "Unfortunately, I haven't time to read your draft now. You can leave it, if you like." He indicated an empty corner of his desk where the folder might be set down. "I won't be able to get to it for several weeks." He did not dare dismiss the boy altogether, because he had not yet taken time to find out exactly who he was.

"Thanks, Mr. Clawsen. I should have some feedback from Senator Pell and Mr. Kissinger by then, so we can compare notes."

Clawsen picked up the folder and stared at it. "Compare notes," he repeated, "with Claiborne Pell and Henry Kissinger."

"That'll be great, won't it?" The boy smiled as he left. "And good luck with the search committee. I hope you find what you're looking for."

THREE

I T WAS THE FIRST DANK WEEK of December and the bone-chilling sleet continued to fall. Indian summer had lasted through Election Day, Margaret Donahue remembered. Dahlias, trellised roses, wild asters that filled every vacant lot with lavender haze, even the blue chicory that grew along the trolley tracks—they were all flowering as people went to the polls and the mercury hit seventy. Then, vengefully, the weather changed: New England had dallied with beauty too long and repented its lapse.

Margaret swore under her breath as she looked for a parking place. It was a nuisance coming back for this open house, but Emory Stokes had urged her not to miss it. Informal gatherings were crucial, he said, to the workings of a search committee. Margaret would have shown up, most likely, without his urging. The Center for Participatory Politics offered its fellows wine and cheese and glimpses of its faculty on Thursday afternoons between five and seven, and Margaret went dutifully almost every week. The people she represented, the Newnham Teachers Federation, were underpaid and imperfectly connected with established powers. Some good might eventually come to them and their pupils through the contacts she made at Marvell.

She was returning from a maddening meeting in Newnham, the city where she lived and worked and for which she felt responsible and a little defensive. A fatuous young man, a ponytailed countercultural kindergarten teacher, had been chosen to represent an elementary school on the board of the union local she had headed for years. He had been feeling, he said—and, oh, Lord, how infinitely she preferred people who thought, or at any rate prefaced their suggestions with the claim that they had done so—he felt that the union had not devoted itself sufficiently to the personal and spiritual growth of its members and proposed weekends of sensitivity training and meditation. He actually referred to these sessions as retreats.

This delegate had taken the place of an appalling malingerer who dreamed of modeling teachers' hours and benefits on those already conceded to employees in the department of public works. Margaret had fought him tooth and nail, and won; he'd left teaching and found a job with the county, but had been replaced by this wimp, this sharing and caring wimp. Margaret had just about given up on the idea of progress. She wished she had gone straight home after the meeting. She might be at home now in a hot bath, thinking about her editorial for next week's newsletter.

She spotted a woman lengthily extracting car keys from a shoulder bag and moved her car into position. An alarmed look crossed the woman's face; probably a harried Christmas shopper who'd left a package somewhere, she rushed off on foot. Margaret swore again and moved on. She got out at a traffic light to scrape the frozen sleet from her windshield wipers, but before she'd finished, the light changed. Horns shrieked as she climbed back in and moved her car cautiously forward.

Incompetence, vagueness, the talk of the meeting maddened her, and the talk of the Center would be no less self-serving and insubstantial. The idiom was different, the impulses were not. Margaret swung her car into a space that

opened up near the Center and hurried inside. She took off
her coat in the ladies' room and stared uncharitably at herself
in the mirror. Her hair was more gray than black, her nose
red and her bright blue eyes sunken and peevish. She
brushed the sleet from her hair, powdered her sharp nose
and went out into the common room.

"You look half-frozen," someone said. "Aren't you used to
the cold?" She recognized him as Jake Larson, the man from
the UAW. Larson seldom spoke in their labor history class,
but when he did he said interesting things.

"Resigned to it," she answered, "but not immune."

"Wait right here. You need some *glogg.*" He returned a
minute later with a steaming cup, and she sipped it gratefully. "The winters start early in Michigan too," he said. "But
we'd have snow by now and it's prettier."

"Ah, Ms. Donahue," Emory Stokes joined them. "I'm glad
to see you've already met Mr. Larson. You'll be working
closely together and, of course, very closely with us too."

"Working on what?" Margaret asked.

"The search committee, of course. I'm so delighted you're
here. Two of my colleagues are clamoring to meet you." He
beckoned to a frail, balding man who stood, apparently await-
ing his summons. "Ms. Donahue, Margaret, Alvin Worth. Alvin, you've met Jake Larson? Alvin's our leading expert on
bureaucratic ethics. He insists it's not a contradiction in
terms."

Worth smiled wanly. "I get a certain amount of chaffing
about my field. But I tell them I'd rather be a living oxymoron
than a dead one."

"That must silence your critics," Margaret replied, trying
to remember where she'd heard Worth's name before.

Larson established the connection. "You sent me a package
of papers from the search committee, didn't you? Are you the
chairman?"

"Professor Norman Clawsen is chairing the committee. He

should be here shortly." Worth sipped his drink, unaccountably ill-at-ease. "I was wondering if either of you'd had a chance as yet to glance at any of the candidates' materials. You should have received a packet also, Miss Donahue. If any of it seems too technical—" he paused; it sounded condescending. "If you encounter unfamiliar terms, I'd be only too happy to interpret. I know Professor Clawsen wants to be available to you, too . . ." He glanced nervously around the room. Where could Norman be? Had he forgotten the open house?

"I read an article last night," Margaret said. "It was perfectly clear to me, and I thought very insightful."

"Do you recall the author's name?" Worth took another small sip.

"I bet it was Richard Llewellyn." Jake Larson said. "His paper about teachers, preachers and Populist oratory is great."

"It was Llewellyn," she recalled. "But another paper, about a cooperative dairy that stamped Progressive slogans on its cheese rinds. It was wonderful."

"I was afraid the reading would be pretty dull," Larson admitted. "But I'm really enjoying it."

"I'm delighted to hear it." Worth, who did not appear overcome with the delight he professed, saw Norman Clawsen enter the room and managed to catch his eye.

Clawsen made his practiced way through the crowd. "Business as well as pleasure being transacted here?" he asked. "Are these the new fellows?" He introduced himself affably but, more inclined to business than pleasure, spent little time in small talk. "So," he said, "you've both agreed to serve on my search committee?"

"The search has gained two very conscientious members, Norman." Worth warned his friend. "Conscientious *and enthusiastic.*"

"Enthusiastic about anything or anyone in particular?"

Clawsen feared he knew the answer to his question, but he saw no alternative to asking it.

Margaret sensed his disapproval. "I'm keeping an open mind. It happens that we, Jake Larson and I, both started on Richard Llewellyn's papers first, and we both liked his work."

"It is, undeniably, accessible," Worth acknowledged.

"There is another candidate who attempts rather more," Clawsen said. "You may find his work more—" he paused. He realized he couldn't tell them they would not understand the dissertation. He plunked for "challenging" at the same moment Worth supplied "ambitious."

"And that young man will be here on Monday," Worth continued. "You might defer reading his thesis until you've heard his oral presentation."

"He'll be here at the same time as Llewellyn then?" Larson asked.

"We may ask him to stay on," Worth said. "Richard Llewellyn is coming the week after next."

"But he's here now," Larson said. "I met him in Sam Sternberg's office fifteen minutes ago."

"Is that Llewellyn?" Margaret asked. Sam Sternberg was introducing a young man to Caleb Tuttle, the Center's venerable dean. Richard Llewellyn was pleasant looking, she thought, lean and alert, with dark hair and fresh-colored skin, and a thin black Irish face that, Margaret supposed, Welsh ancestry might equally well have furnished.

"Did you get the date wrong?" Clawsen asked when the dean brought Llewellyn over to meet them.

"We were looking forward to seeing you later this month." Worth managed a more hospitable greeting.

"I'm looking forward to it, too," Llewellyn answered easily.

"And what brings you to Marvell today?"

"I met Mrs. Sternberg at Yale, at a colloquium on peasants. She's interested in migrant laborers, and we got to talking and she suggested I drive back with her and have a look at Marvell."

"A happy coincidence." Worth smiled and drained his glass.

"I'm happy to be here, and it's just as easy to fly from Boston as New York," Llewellyn said. "Can I get you another drink?"

"Thank you." Worth gave him his glass. "A very weak scotch, please. The bartender knows my brand."

"More *glogg,* Margaret?" Larson asked.

"No, thanks," she said. "But I'll walk over to the bar with you. I see an old student of mine."

"Which one?"

"The pretty one talking with Emory Stokes. She dropped out of high school and I was pleased to find her here looking so well." Donna Franchetti's abrupt departure from Newnham High School had pained Margaret, hardened as she was to the facts of working-class adolescence.

"Miss Donahue," Donna Franchetti greeted her warmly. "Mr. Stokes told me to be sure to come to the wine-and-cheese today. He promised me you'd be here, too."

"Fact is," Stokes said, "there are too few women at the Center and too damn few pretty ones."

"But you do everything in your power to attract them," Larson said.

"Attract them to the Center, you mean? I certainly do everything I can. I am one of the few sincere feminists in this institution." Stokes's speech was slightly slurred. He had been drinking steadily since four-thirty.

"What are you studying?" Richard Llewellyn asked. He had delivered Worth's drink and returned to the bar.

"I work in the library," she said. A girl more intelligent than most who left school, more promising, Margaret had always thought, than many who graduated, Donna Franchetti had survived the damaging rashness of young love and now was divorcing the abusive loser she'd married at seventeen.

"What kind of employer is Marvell?" Jake Larson asked her, but Emory Stokes replied. "Oh, it's splendid. Great benefits. Great health program. Great tuition reductions for the staff—Donna's taking advantage of them. Great . . ."

Stokes's encomium was cut short by an angry young man in soiled sodden coveralls, rain dripping from his disheveled hair. "Donna," the intruder spoke throatily, "you're comin' home with me. Now."

"No," she said.

"How did you get in here?" Emory Stokes was surprised by this interruption. Controversial personages visited the Center almost daily. Elaborate precautions had been taken in the building's construction; security remained, after salaries and entertainment, the costliest item in the Center's budget. Although unauthorized entry had been made virtually impossible, help was always close at hand. Stokes backed away and pressed an unobtrusive gray button on the common-room wall.

The man's coveralls identified him as an employee of a local brewery. "You came in through the delivery entrance, didn't you?" Larson asked. He was a tall man, big-boned and slow-moving, and as he spoke, he stepped deliberately closer to Donna.

"Yeah, what of it?" Franchetti stepped forward also. "I ain't leavin' without my wife."

"We're separated, Tommy. We're getting a divorce." Donna Franchetti said this dully, as if she had said it many times. "I'm not going anywhere with you."

"Come on, son," Larson said. "I'll walk you back to your truck."

Sidestepping Larson, Franchetti lunged at Donna. Richard Llewellyn caught him by the wrist and spun him toward Larson, who grasped his other arm. Franchetti, pinned between them, muttered threats as they walked him out of the common room and into the custody of security guards rushing to answer the alarm.

Margaret had snatched Donna out of Franchetti's reach the moment he sprang, and she released her only after the guards had taken him away. "I'll drive you home when you're ready to leave," she said. "Where are you living now?"

"Downstairs from my mother. Don't worry, Miss Donahue, I'll be okay."

"I'm sure you'll be fine. But when you want to leave, I'll be happy to drop you off."

"I think Miss Donahue's concern is well-founded," Emory Stokes said. "I'd be pleased to escort you myself."

Donna thanked him but declined. "I live very close to Miss Donahue," she explained.

"It's on my way, really." Margaret was certain Stokes ought not to be driving that evening. "That was pretty slick," she said as Larson and Llewellyn rejoined them. "I'm glad you two were here."

"So am I," Donna said. "Thank you." Franchetti embarrassed her more than he frightened her, and she hated to talk about him. She hated even to think about him, so she left her gratitude largely unspoken. Llewellyn, too, seemed happy to speak of other things and turned his attention from her only to accept the dean's thanks.

"Neatly done," Caleb Tuttle laid his hand briefly on the young man's shoulder. "You saved us an ugly ruckus. No more force than was needed but no less." Tuttle gave praise sparingly and his support counted for much at the Center. Emory Stokes thought the search was just about over until he saw the look that Alvin Worth and Norman Clawsen exchanged and concluded they would not accept defeat easily.

After Llewellyn left in haste to make his plane, Jake Larson said he'd like to come along when Margaret drove Donna home. He saw the young woman to the door of her second-floor apartment, noting that people seemed to be at home in the apartments above and beneath her and leaving her only after she assured him that, of course, she'd had the locks changed.

"Come see a movie with me," he said as he got back into Margaret's car. "I think she'll be all right."

"I'd like to, but I've got to write an editorial for our news-letter. Nobody's filling in for me in the local. I'm sorry."

"Reprint an old one," he suggested. "You've had a long day."

"Okay. There's that old standby, the alternatives to merit pay. That's always timely."

AUDREY CLAWSEN WISHED, as she watched the second hand on the kitchen clock, that she had never met her husband or that she had thought things through more clearly. A letter had come that morning from her mother, mentioning, as her mother's letters so often did, that her old boyfriend, who had been so crazy about her in high school, continued to prosper.

"Audrey, are these eggs fresh?"

"I bought them yesterday."

"Where?"

"At Mallory's."

"Not at the supermarket?"

"No, at Mallory's," she repeated. "They're fresher there, at least, they usually are. You can't count on anything anymore."

"You're right about that anyway," her husband replied. "I'll butter the toast myself. You always make it too greasy."

Audrey never understood why women bragged about their husbands' helping in the kitchen. Norman drove her almost wild with his fussing. And on days when something went wrong, he could eat only soft-boiled eggs for supper, and not even those unless, as he always said, "you can manage not to harden the yolks so that they are entirely inedible. It's a simple enough task, God knows." He sometimes added, "Any moron could watch the clock and take the eggs out two minutes after the water starts to boil again." She did not ask him how his day had been on the nights when he asked for soft-boiled eggs. Something must have gone wrong at the Center that day, because he talked to himself as he ate his eggs.

"Oh, damn, and the dean saw the whole thing," he was saying, "and acted as if Llewellyn had saved a batallion. And Stokes chiming in about *sang froid* . . ." Preoccupied as he was, he ate fastidiously. She had found that, at one time, so refined. "But I can count on Alvin. Bert Harding won't give a damn one way or the other. Oh, God, I'm tired."

"Would you like a cup of tea, Norman?" she asked hesitantly.

"No, I'm going straight to bed. I've got to get up early and write some letters." He rose from the table. She turned her cheek to him for a kiss, but he ignored her and went upstairs.

When she was sure he was asleep, she poured herself a small glass of Grand Marnier and sat down with *House and Garden*. Just a little glass. Alcohol upset Norman's stomach, so they rarely had drinks before or after dinner, but she needed a little something to relax her so she could sleep. Her mind wandered as she leafed through the magazine, imagining what it would be like to live in a house like those houses, with a man who said when he came home, "Audrey, I don't know how you do it. Every time I come home the house is spotless, dinner is wonderful, and you get more beautiful all the time." And then she'd sit on his lap in a big chair in front of the fire while they had a drink, or if it was summertime they'd sit by the pool. And, after they ate dinner, he'd say, "Leave the dishes, sweetheart, we've got better things to do." And he'd start unbuttoning her blouse as they went upstairs.

She poured herself another drink. She wondered if Norman would, as he had promised, take her to England with him next spring. He had been invited to a conference in a city with a romantic name, Newcastle upon Tyne. She knew it was in the northern part of the country; she had found it on a map and hoped it would be near a moor or a heath. If he let her come with him, she would first go shopping at Talbots. She imagined her conversation with the saleslady: "My husband has been asked to deliver a paper," she would begin and then add casually, "in the United Kingdom." The woman would be impressed and say, "How nice." That's all she'd say: "How nice." It was a good store and the salespeople did not gush the way they did at outlets, but she would be impressed. And then she'd ask, "Are you going to accompany him? Can you get away yourself?" And Audrey would say, "Yes, he wants me at his side." She wondered how much Norman would let her spend on a suit.

"Audrey! Audrey!" his querulous voice broke into her reverie. He always did that, just lay in bed and called for her. "Where's the thermometer? I think I have a fever. I never have a headache as bad as this unless I have a temperature too."

FOUR

HE CENTER DEALT CONFIDENTLY with hypothetical dangers. Its associates refought, in weekly role-playing exercises, many classic battles; they spun out scenarios for conventional and nuclear wars—preemptive, simultaneous and retaliatory strikes—with iron logic and alarming specificity. Faced with Tommy Franchetti, the Center looked for more practical help. It installed more video cameras and monitors, hired additional security guards and called Polaroid. By three o'clock of the day following the disturbance, all nonfaculty employees had been issued photo IDs.

Franchetti had found a chink in the armor; in response, new procedures were put in place, the cares delegated and forgotten. Margaret Donahue, however, could not so easily set aside her fears. She worried through the short winter's day and, in the sullen dusk, remained troubled. Donna wouldn't always be at Marvell, surrounded by cool-headed friends. Margaret flipped through her Rolodex. Nick Hannibal, Molly Rafferty's fiancé, might have a word of advice. Nick worked in Boston, but he lived in Newnham, where he'd grown up and, Margaret knew, kept his eyes open wherever he was. The man who answered the phone in the Homicide Unit said Lt. Hannibal had just left. He didn't think he'd be going home. Hadn't she heard about the torso in the dinghy? No, having skipped the *Herald* that morning, she'd missed both torso and dinghy. She left her name, then tried his home number, hoping to find Molly. Molly had sublet her own place in anticipation of a now postponed leave of absence and moved in with Nick for the rest of the semester.

"How are you?" Molly recognized her voice. "And how's Marvell?"

"All you said it would be and more."

"Why don't you come for supper and tell us about it? Nick's rushing home for a bite to eat and then out again. The Coast Guard found something grisly floating off Deer Island."

Nick was at the door to greet her. "Anything wrong, Margaret?" He's looking well, she thought; he gave an impression of sensual well-being, perfectly complete, but active, unsated.

"Probably nothing much." She had a great fear of appearing alarmist. "Did you ever know Tom Franchetti, unpleasant kid, arrested a couple of times for assault?"

"I'd recognize him if I saw him. Have you told Molly any of this yet? She'll want to hear about it, too." They settled companionably around the kitchen table while Molly did one thing and another in some orderly sequence of chopping, draining and whisking that she seemed to have fixed in her head and that Margaret, who wasn't much of a cook, could not follow. From time to time, she sipped a glass of wine Nick handed her.

"They're separated," Margaret concluded her story, "and Donna's doing very well on her own. But it was mortifying for her."

"Did he hit her?" Nick asked, moving a plate of cheese and radishes closer to Margaret and refilling her glass.

"He tried to grab her, but he was hustled away before he got to her."

"And she was a protegée of yours at the high school?" He hazarded a guess. Margaret, like Molly, was fiercely protective of her students. "I'm surprised you didn't deck him yourself. Are you sure you need help?"

"I thought you'd have a sense about how worried I ought to be."

"I'll ask around." He took a heavy casserole from Molly and carried it into the dining room. "She's a level-headed young woman?" he asked Margaret as he seated her.

"None leveler."

"It doesn't sound too bad. I'll check into it and call you in a day or two."

She knew he would. Like the better politicians, Nick Hannibal followed through.

"Who hustled Franchetti out so expeditiously?" Molly asked, passing Margaret a plate of stew. It had lamb and barley and tiny vegetables in it and looked very good.

"The UAW troubleshooter, who looked as though he'd shot worse trouble than Tommy, and Richard Llewellyn, one of the candidates the search committee's interviewing."

"Richard Llewellyn, really?" Molly was pleasantly surprised. "He's a very hot property in American social history. It's astonishing the poli-sci crowd agreed to interview him. Have I missed his talk?"

"He's scheduled for later this month," Margaret said. "And I'm glad he was there yesterday." She sounded as if she thought the trouble wasn't over.

"Margaret"—Nick knew she took most crises in her stride —"why are you so worried about this?"

"Franchetti was expelled from the trade high school at the height of the squabble over metal detectors. He was caught with a knife and suspended. The very day he came back, he attacked a younger boy during recess."

"You took a hard line then." Hannibal remembered the ferocity of that debate. The school committee had consulted him informally and he'd advised against installing the devices.

"Some people thought it was the soft line," she recalled. "I said we should expel the known troublemakers and use the money for something the school really needed. The trade school is prisonlike enough as it is." Margaret's agenda for Newnham included phasing out the vocational school altogether and bringing its students into a comprehensive high school. "The voc-tech kids don't need any more degrading experiences. Very few boys ever brought weapons to school."

"And those who did," Nick added, "usually hid them in garbage cans or dumpsters around the playground and never took them into the building at all. They used them mostly at recess."

"The way you say Franchetti did. Do they have children?" Molly asked.

"Two."

"She knows about the Family Abuse Prevention Act?" Nick suggested. Courts acted fairly quickly these days to restrain troublesome spouses.

"She hasn't applied for a court order yet. I did mention it, but he seems just to watch her, to keep an eye on her from a distance."

"She should file anyway. It'll make it easier to pick him up the next time he makes trouble for her."

"Is she ambivalent about him, do you think?" Molly asked. "Does she want him back? Or want him to show her how much he wants her back?"

"She's not the least bit ambivalent," Margaret answered emphatically, although the idea hadn't crossed her mind. She considered it now and rejected it. "I am sure she's completely fed up with him and eager to prove she doesn't need any help, apart from the process of divorce, to get rid of him."

"Do you know what the fight was about?" Nick asked. "The one that got him thrown out of school?"

"The younger kid was Haitian."

"But was it a girl, or dope, or money, or wouldn't he let Franchetti copy his homework?"

"Since when do they assign homework down there?" Margaret replied. "It was simple xenophobia."

"Xenophobia's rarely simple," Molly said. "There's got to be a precipitating event. The Haitians are there every day."

"I can't remember." Margaret was annoyed with herself. "This dinner's so pleasant, I'm stupid with contentment."

"It's not important," Nick said. "I was curious about what gets to Franchetti. People don't change all that much."

"Tell us about Marvell." Molly had a weakness for academic gossip. "Do strange men still come up to you and tell you their college board scores?"

"Now that you mention it," Margaret could think of several who had. "I should have known it wasn't my peculiar charm that drove them to do it."

"Men try their pathetic best to impress you," Nick said, bringing in the salad for Molly to toss. "You shouldn't scoff."

"I bet you never told Molly yours."

"Actually," Molly smiled, "it came up in the most natural way when we were talking about where his high school classmates applied to college."

"And after, I hope, I'd impressed you in other ways."

"Oh, you had. You didn't lead with your test results."

"Why didn't you go to Marvell?" Margaret asked him. "The admissions office has asked me several times already to encourage more applicants from Newnham."

"They're dead earnest about diversity," Molly agreed. "That's one goal they really care about."

"So it seemed. I thought their recruiter was condescending," Nick recalled. "Here we were at Boston College High, a tough academic school with a classical curriculum. The woman who came from the University of Chicago talked to us about Aristotle. The Marvell guy just wanted to talk about ethnicity. He was delighted my father was born in Italy, but he seemed disappointed my mother came from Plymouth. I was pretty full of myself then and I thought I could offer more than local color."

"Oh, but, Nick," Molly was looking at him with the most evident pleasure, "such color . . ." His eyes held hers for a minute before the lower part of his face smiled. The irony that played over his face saved him, Margaret thought, from the banality of simply being darkly handsome. Who knew if his face would be brooding in repose? You never saw him when he didn't appear to be thinking.

"You're so pale and ladylike," he said. "Everybody looks colorful to you."

"The science fair," Margaret said. Molly was making coffee by depressing a silvery plunger in a glass pot. The gleaming apparatus and Molly's gesture, like detonating a charge, brought back to her the answer to Nick's question. "Cléo, the Haitian boy Franchetti attacked, built an electric engine for a moped. Usually only the college-prep students do projects for the science fair, but this boy was too new to know that, so he mailed in the design on his own."

"And he won and got lots of glory?" Molly loved true stories about the American dream. She had grown up in a prosperous suburb, and, in college and in graduate school at Marvell, she'd made a point of avoiding dim young men from privileged backgrounds. What, she sometimes thought in declining their invitations, did they think that I came here to do? "Did he actually get to the finals?"

"He got an honorable mention at the state level. It was a big day for the Haitians. The mayor and his state rep and the pastor of the Nouvelle Eglise all came to the awards ceremony. And Cléo got himself switched to the high school and enrolled in algebra and chemistry. All that was so much more exciting than the fight with Tommy Franchetti, I'd forgotten it happened to the same boy."

"He wasn't seriously hurt then?" Nick asked.

"No, but only because he had sense enough to run away. The minute he saw the knife he took off, and a tough phys-ed teacher tackled Franchetti before he caught up with him."

"Franchetti's goat is gotten by academic success, and his estranged wife's at Marvell?" Molly cut an apple and apricot tart. "Terrific."

FIVE

"**B**UT IT MUST BE someone pushing back the frontiers of political science." Norman Clawsen's slight body trembled with the force of his conviction. The committee had been cool the previous afternoon to a candidate from whom he expected great things. "He, he or she, must be at the cutting edge."

"What he or she should be cutting," Sam Sternberg said, "is the crap. The more data they collect, the less it matters. And that's the only correlation, Norman, that impressed me in yesterday's performance."

"But sample size is crucial," Clawsen insisted. He resented Sternberg's participation in what was, after all, a political science search. "Everything hinges on the n."

"Remind me, would you, Norman, what n stands for?" Caleb Tuttle asked. Tuttle, the dean of the Center, was sitting in on this meeting because he'd heard the committee was close to an impasse.

"N," Clawsen explained patiently, "is the total number of subjects interviewed or episodes analyzed, the basic sum of whatever it is that is the subject of the research. It is a concept basic to the methodology with which political science is making such gigantic strides." He elaborated because Tuttle was vastly influential. Everyone at the Center deferred to him, Clawsen knew; some to his official position, others to his formidable person.

"Yes, thank you, you put it very clearly. And that last talk rested, certainly, on considerable research and gave us much, uh, much food for thought," Tuttle replied, fingering the knot of his Marvell College tie in courteous hesitation; the tie, a rich purple silk, was speckled with the golden logo, an *M* intertwined with the four *V*s of the college motto, *Vel virtus vel vis.* The motto meant "Either virtue or power," and Clawsen reckoned men like Tuttle wielded both might and right, whichever the occasion demanded. "But, Norman," the dean was saying, "I do think Sam has a point."

Damn it, Clawsen thought, Sternberg had gotten to him first. Yankees and Jews, that unholy alliance, things at Marvell increasingly worked that way. And Sternberg's wife was Tuttle's second cousin or grandniece or godchild or whatever.

"I doubt that I'm on the cutting edge myself, Norman," Tuttle went on in his modest, reasonable way, "but I've read everything the people on your shortlist sent us, and, frankly, with one exception, its significance escapes me. What's your objection to the young man who works on agrarian radicalism?"

"Richard Llewellyn? He's a history and literature type."

"He does write well." The dean agreed.

"But Llewellyn is by nobody's standard a political scientist, Caleb, merely a historian. We don't want a historian for this job, do we?"

"I never understood where history stopped and politics began," Tuttle replied. "I found his work very perceptive."

"Llewellyn's coming in a few days, Norm," Sam said. "Can't we discuss him after we've heard him?"

"This committee has been hypercritical of *many* able young scholars," Clawsen replied. He had scheduled Llewellyn last because he'd expected a clear favorite, vastly superior to the historian, to emerge from the earlier sessions. "Happily, I know of a truly innovative young man at Rice we've overlooked."

"Fine," Sternberg said. "Get him here as soon as you can."

"Perhaps we might make the midcareer fellows voting members of the search," Tuttle suggested.

Screw them both, Clawsen thought, enraged by further evidence of collusion. Sternberg had proposed that too, at the outset. The Center dealt with practical politics, he'd argued, and its associates had a responsibility to make themselves intelligible to lay people. He reminded them that the Center's brochure, written, as everyone knew, by Norman Clawsen himself, put forth as the Center's chief purpose "to facilitate dialogue enhancement and to optimize interface between the academy and the polity." Clawsen had labored to get the phrasing right, and that passage was one he had lingered over and loved. He liked it very much less when Sternberg read it aloud and said he could not have put it better. It eloquently expressed his own hopes. And, since they were all in agreement, wouldn't it be a good idea to involve the fellows?

"Input, certainly, we welcome input, Caleb. But these people are not scholars. Suppose they liked somebody we could not possibly appoint . . . Don't you see what a can of worms we'd have opened up?"

Earlier that fall, Clawsen had simply beaten back Sternberg's proposal, but he could not dismiss the dean so easily. Besides, two men who agreed with him were unavailable that afternoon, and Emory Stokes would never object to anything Tuttle proposed. Stokes was a toady who prided himself on his worldliness. "Their expertise is, of course, invaluable, in many ways," he conceded. "But I cannot believe it would be appropriate to grant them a vote in faculty appointments."

"The faculty retain a clear majority, Norman, unless they are seriously divided," Tuttle reminded him. "And I do think it would help all of us, since political science seems to be moving into rather, uh, heady realms, to make sure that the candidates can—how did you put it in our prospectus—make themselves heard in the forum?"

"Interface with the polity." Clawsen's phrase pleased him less and less.

"Exactly," Tuttle said.

"But we can't change procedures in the middle of a search." Clawsen's voice grew shrill with exasperation.

"We aren't in the middle of a search," Sternberg said. "We're back at square one. We've eliminated some turkeys and we've got Llewellyn and your hotshot from Rice coming up. If anybody looks good in retrospect, we can ask him back. Let's adjourn, Norman. I haven't had dinner with my wife all week. I'd like to get home."

Clawsen, his body inclined, his head nodding in supplication, escorted Tuttle to the Center's front desk and waited with him while the security guard called a cab.

"Don't be too discouraged, Norman," the dean said. "These searches have tiresome moments. Was none of the women candidates interesting?"

"Marvell asks its faculty to be a bit more than 'interesting,' doesn't it?" Clawsen began to feel sick.

"Nearly half our graduate students are women," Tuttle persisted, "and I don't think the national figures are any lower. It's odd the committee's seeing only young men. Ah, here's my cab. Good night, Norman."

Clawsen walked abstractedly to the office of his friend, Alvin Worth. Worth was thoroughly reliable; he rarely skipped a committee meeting, and he'd missed this one only because he'd been obliged to conduct a thesis defense. Clawsen sought him out whenever he felt agitated. They understood each other: each believed that he and the other man shouldered more than their fair share of departmental duties. Some of their colleagues were celebrities; a few were schol-

ars. Clawsen and Alvin Worth were neither, and they envied
the stars far more than they even professed to respect the
thinkers, whom they regarded with almost total incompre-
hension.

The students, they agreed, though they seldom spoke
about them, were wiseassed brats of two equally repellent
sorts: the graceful ones preparing to assume positions members of their families traditionally occupied and the keen-
eyed overachievers running hard to break in. Clawsen de-
tested them all; suavity and energy alike irritated him, and
even sycophancy had begun to pall. He tried not to think
about students much, but their presence intruded on him.
And he did not trust any of them. He always kept his office
door open when meeting with male as well as with female
students: charges of sexual harassment were, after all, almost
impossible to disprove. Even if the kid turned out to be certi-
fiable, somebody could say you caused the breakdown.

Worth, though uncommunicative, got on better with students; his silence prompted them to speak, and they mistook
his moroseness for interested sympathy. His lugubrious reti-
cence cheered Clawsen too. Worth rarely spoke above a
strained whisper, and his mannered speech made Clawsen's
own nervous garrulity seem fluent and candid.

"He asked why there were no women on the shortlist."

"We should have had one. You remember that other
time . . ."

Clawsen remembered. Neither of them was likely to forget
that debacle. Some years before, a woman who ran a neighborhood pediatric clinic and day care center in Milwaukee
had applied for a fellowship. They had put her application
unread into the affirmative action file that they kept should
they be required to produce at short notice more of any dis-
advantaged group than they had at the moment on hand. Her
papers had lain undisturbed until she won a Pulitzer prize
for a critical biography of Maria Montessori. Some of those

publicity-seeking bastards at Marvell's Institute for Health and Society found out she had applied to the Center. She was a registered nurse, so they claimed her as potentially their own, and they'd raised a terrific stink that the dossier had not been forwarded to them.

"Have you become a libertarian, Norman?" Caleb Tuttle had asked him. His earnest, soft voice conveyed that he was trying to give you the benefit of the doubt but you weren't making it easy for him.

"How then," the dean had continued after Clawsen's mumbled negative, "if it was not principled noncompliance, do you justify your mockery of this law? We are committed to the proposition that the state can, under certain circumstances, promote the general good. The Center itself is explicitly committed to nondiscriminatory recruitment. I remember when you yourself wrote compellingly of movements for social justice. Norman, this is a disgrace. Please make sure nothing like it happens again."

Clawsen had gone home and thrown up after the old man had finished with him. He was fighting back nausea now as he grappled with the current problem. "We'll see some more candidates. We'll schedule more sessions and pack them. Emory Stokes will go anywhere liquor is served, but I doubt Bert Harding will attend many more."

"Bert told me before he left the country that he would under no circumstances attend more than three job talks. He asked me how many synopses of how many dash-dash-dash-dashing dissertations I expected him to sit through in one term. You know how he affects coarse language." Worth sighed reproachfully.

"He doesn't have to come to any of the talks. I'd be glad if he didn't, but he'll make sure he's there to vote. He doesn't want anybody brought here who doesn't owe him something."

"I don't think a man who's missed more than two

presentations should be permitted to vote," Worth objected, and conscious of the unimpeachable fairness of his judgment, he continued primly. "It would not hurt Bertram Harding to concern himself a bit more with the business of the Center. We do pay half his salary." Bert Harding divided his time between the Center and Marvell's political science department.

"He's worth much more to us than we pay him, Al," Clawsen reminded his friend. "Bert really rakes it in. Every time he has a piece in the *New York Times Magazine,* the checks start rolling in on Tuesday morning. He knows that. We all do. And, don't forget, Al, he never fails to describe himself as an associate of the Center."

"You are more than humanly generous, Norman. And Bert would be the man to find us a woman, if the dean really wants to see one. The boy from Rice was a good idea. His advisor thinks he'll get two or three articles out of his thesis. He's a real go-getter. And perhaps," Worth mulled over a strategem, "we might also hear that Thai from USC. What do you think about him?"

"He's an oddball. He doesn't speak English, and I heard he didn't say a word in Thai until he was fifteen."

"Perhaps not. He relies, I believe, on mathematical notation. His appearance at the American Political Science Convention last summer caused a minor sensation. You must remember it—something about permutations of margins of error in attitudinal surveys."

"Ah, the cutting edge," Clawsen intoned, "the cutting edge of the discipline."

"Mercy, Norman, I don't want to hire him. I simply want to acquaint the others with the direction of future inquiry, with, shall we say, the discipline's trajectory."

"You mean you want to freak them out. That's a damn good idea. You're sharp, Alvin." Clawsen snickered with relief. The prospect of his colleagues' discomfiture—Emory

Stokes, uncomprehending, pretending to scrutinize the equations; the boistrous Bertram Harding reduced to fidgeting; Sam Sternberg, who would never be rude to a newcomer, trying surreptitiously to turn pages in the book on his lap—the prospect was balm to him. "I saw him at the convention. He's a zombie. Next to Tikibooboo or whatever his name is, the kid from Rice sounds like," Clawsen searched his memory for some exemplar of English prose, "like Ted Sorenson," he concluded after a few moments' reflection.

"I'll trust your judgment there, Norman, and as to the fellows' voting, I think it might prove a blessing in disguise. They're not burdened with too much formal education. They'll rely on our judgment."

"I don't like that noisy little man from the International Ladies Garment Workers Union. He'll follow Sternberg's lead. Those New Yorkers stick together."

Worth acquiesced uncomfortably. Clawsen's prejudices were a little too close to the surface. "Yes, but that quiet Swede can be lobbied. And that woman, the schoolteacher."

"Frustrated old maid, probably a man-hater."

"She's rather acerbic. She does collective bargaining." Worth continued soothingly. "That goes far to explain Miss Donahue's manner. But what can she know about political science? We'll take her to lunch at the Faculty Club."

SIX

EORGE GRESHAM, finishing his doctoral dissertation at Rice, did not hesitate when Marvell University summoned him. He canceled three other job interviews to prepare for his appearance there, but, despite his best efforts, he failed to make an impression. His talk sounded a little over-rehearsed, and he did not handle questions well; Gresham seemed, in fact, not always to grasp what he was being asked. But he had done his homework: he found occasion to mention at least two books written by everyone present, the most famous and the most recent.

He called them all "Professor" except Emory Stokes, whom he addressed as "Mr. Secretary." And that really was remarkable, because few people remembered that Stokes had served, for some months in 1953, as acting assistant deputy under-secretary of commerce. It had come about because the man Eisenhower wanted to appoint, a wholesale hardware dealer called back to active duty with the Ohio National Guard, refused to leave Korea until all his POWs were accounted for; Stokes had schemed unsuccessfully, ever since the colonel's return, to regain cabinet rank. Sam Sternberg said George Gresham had a great future in fund-raising: he'd be an asset to the Center in that capacity if in no other.

Bertram Harding missed Gresham's talk and strode, badly

sunburned, into Norman Clawsen's office on the eve of Llewellyn's presentation. "Plane was held up overnight in Cairo and three more hours in Rome. How'd the new one look?"

"I thought he acquitted himself very well, but Sternberg and the dean didn't like him. And the midcareer fellows, who are now voting members of the search in consequence of some machinations that took place in your absence, put questions to him he might have answered better."

"If Sam and Caleb don't like him, he's a nonstarter. Christ, Norman, why do we have to invite so many? I wouldn't spend this long picking Miss Universe."

"The end is in sight," he said. "We've asked Gresham to stay for a few days. And I think you will agree with most of us in preferring him to Llewellyn, who's performing tomorrow."

"Okay, bring 'em on and may the best man win," Harding said. "When's dinner? I've had nothing to eat all day but some fiddling scampi. Would you believe it—they ran out of steak in first class?"

"Shortly," Clawsen replied. "I have some matters to discuss with you."

The search committee was dining that evening with both candidates; by the time Clawsen and Harding arrived at the Faculty Club, the others had gathered in the library for drinks. Sam Sternberg and Jake Larson were listening as George Gresham swapped smutty stories about Texas politicians, local and national, with Emory Stokes. Richard Llewellyn sat on a leather sofa with Alvin Worth, who was expounding some theme evidently dear to his heart; Llewellyn, with equal seriousness, asked questions to which Worth replied with diminishing patience. Lou Stillman, who had spent most of the previous night preventing a wildcat strike of Hispanic blouse finishers, dozed in an armchair. Margaret Donahue had excused herself: the school committee was meeting that evening and she thought she'd better be there.

"How was your trip, Bert?" Sam Sternberg rose to welcome Harding.

"Swell. Very productive." Bert Harding asked for a beer and chugged it with exaggerated satisfaction, as though, Clawsen thought, he had been working on the docks all day instead of jetting back from Al Awash.

"And how's our old friend, the emir?" Stokes asked. "Would this be a propitious moment to invite him here?"

Worth interrupted his *tête-à-tête* with Llewellyn to suggest sweetening the invitation with an honorary degree.

"He's a little skittish about leaving home just now," Harding cautioned, signaling a waiter for another beer.

"I should think he's skittish," Clawsen said disapprovingly. "Didn't he oust his predecessor, his own brother, while the man was accepting a doctorate at the LSE?"

"Halfbrother," Harding corrected him. "And the limeys never thought he was up to the job. That's why they got him out of the country." He knocked back his second beer. "I didn't know you followed Middle Eastern affairs, Norm. You always say the feuding there leaves you cold."

"I keep track of other institutions' honoraries." Clawsen looked very angry. "Somebody has to."

"Well, I hope the time'll come when he can travel," Harding said. "He's one hell of a guy. Look what he gave me." He took from his attaché case a long, elaborately tooled morocco sheath. "Great, eh? Looks like a condom for a camel. Wait'll you see what's inside." He laid the scabbard on the table in front of him and withdrew a jeweled dagger. Magnificent emeralds formed a crescent on its hilt, and black opals flashed along the seam where the blade was fitted into the haft.

"Murderous-looking thing." Alvin Worth came forward for

a closer look and ran his index finger lightly along the length of the blade. "And very valuable, I am sure."

"The emir must think you're worth your weight in gems," Clawsen said, sipping his diet ginger ale.

"Yeah," Harding replied easily. He was a flaccid man who thought of himself as robust. "Bedouins are very generous people," he reflected, fondling the dagger. "If I know my honey-pie, she'll want to take this baby right down to Shreve's and have the stones reset, but this one's mine. Bitsy won't get her hot little hands on it."

"It's really beautiful, Bert," Sam Sternberg said.

"Out of the Arabian Nights. May I see it?" Richard Llewellyn took the dagger in both hands, admired it for a moment, and then, to everyone's astonishment, he swung it by the tip, as if to gauge how it might be thrown. "Accurate, too, I'd say."

"Is knife throwing among your extracurricular pursuits, Mr. Llewellyn?" Alvin Worth asked.

"No," Llewellyn said, returning the dagger to Harding, who locked it and its handsome sheath in his case. "But at home everybody has a hunting knife. We have venison for Christmas dinner."

"Nothing like an old-fashioned Christmas," Clawsen reminisced, sounding so genial that Llewellyn said what he'd been reluctant to say the first time they met, when Clawsen had seemed so pointedly hostile.

"You do understand what matters to people, Professor Clawsen. I wish you'd use your influence to keep your first book in print. I had a hard time getting hold of it, but when I did, it was invaluable. It's a, an—" he hesitated.

He's not used to fawning, Sam Sternberg thought, he seems a decent guy. Let's get this over with. "I think they're ready for us," he said. A steward was waiting to move them from the library downstairs to a private dining room.

"An exemplary book," Llewellyn resumed eagerly, walking

next to Clawsen, "ground-breaking. The interviews you did were astonishing. The things people confided to you . . ."

"It's rather dated now, I'm afraid," Clawsen interrupted the tribute. "Political science has progressed beyond those methods. I work with harder data now. And you should too, young man. Look beyond the subjective, son." He paused at the head of the stairway and spoke impressively. "Please, take it from me. I'm a farm boy myself, and when I was starting out in political science, I didn't have anybody to set me straight."

"I'm not a farm boy, Professor Clawsen. My father's a Methodist minister."

"Well, a country boy anyhow, and a Midwesterner. I'm trying to help you, Dick. I haven't kept that book in print, because, frankly, it's trash. It embarrasses me."

"I wouldn't say that about anything you've written, Professor Clawsen," George Gresham interposed, close behind them. "But your first book isn't my favorite either."

"Yes, I'm on much firmer ground in my recent work," Clawsen agreed gratefully. "We're all looking forward to your talk tomorrow, Llewellyn," he said as they entered the dining room and seated themselves. "I hope you have more data now than you were able to show in the draft you sent us."

"I've brought some additional tables," Llewellyn said, trying to get a spoonful of the club's gelatinous madrilene. "And maps, with precinct breakdowns for all the rural counties, from 1896 until 1936."

"Good," Clawsen said. "That's something anyway."

"How many counties?" Gresham asked.

"Twenty-three."

"Not much of an *n*, Professor Clawsen, compared with your latest," Gresham said.

"There are only twenty-three predominantly rural counties in the states I'm studying," Llewellyn reminded them, successful at last in detaching a portion of the jellied soup.

"Then you ought to study something else. Frame questions for which there are answers. Political science demands hypotheses that offer at least the potential for verification, or falsifiability," Clawsen said. "Falsifiability, that's the great thing."

SAM STERNBERG WAS TROUBLED by the evening's tenor and stopped to see Caleb Tuttle on his way home. The dean rarely met with search committees, preferring to let members sort things out a bit among themselves before reporting to him, but he liked to hear how things stood.

"They laid it on with a trowel, Caleb," Sternberg told him, "as Disraeli said one must with royal personages. That's the way the great public universities see Marvell, as vestigial as royalty and as irresistible. It didn't surprise me to see Gresham do it, but I never expected Llewellyn to join in."

"As a matter of fact, Sam," Caleb Tuttle said, "Norman's first book is brilliant. I brought him here as soon as I read it. He wrote it when he was twenty-five, and not a word he's written since comes close, in scholarship or in humanity. It's too bad." He stroked the big gray and white Maine coon cat that lay on the arm of his chair. "Too bad. Did Bert get back all right?"

"Blooming," Sam said. "Red as a beet, bearing emeralds."

"Did he stop over in Cairo?"

"Just overnight."

"So he didn't have a chance to . . ."

"No, apparently not," Sam said. "He saw no one of any importance."

"It's difficult," Caleb Tuttle shook his head. His wife had died many years before and they'd had no children. Sam, his godchild's husband, was very near to a son and the two men were not dissimilar, lean and erect, with high bony foreheads over keen eyes. Though the older man was sturdier and less graceful, they were plainly cast from the same mold, and their resemblance prompted family jokes about earlier unions between Jews and Puritans in Cromwell's Commonwealth or in the tolerant Netherlands.

"Very difficult." Sam agreed and neither spoke for some time. "Bert did see a visiting congressman at the Cairo Hilton." Sam thought Tuttle should hear this. "One of his constituents is finishing a doctorate in politics at some fundamentalist university. She's worked in his office every summer since high school and he thinks the world of her. It seems she'd heard about our search but didn't want anything to do with Marvell."

"She must think we're a little to the left of Sodom and Gomorrah." Tuttle's cat stepped down from the arm of his chair and settled composedly on his lap.

"What else would she think? Bert tells me her dissertation sounded extremely original. He's getting a copy, and if it's as good as it sounds, he thinks we should interview her."

"She'd strike some new notes here," Tuttle said. "We could use that."

"Bert's prepared to embrace diversity."

"Don't underestimate him, Sam."

SEVEN

"'P ASTA IS AN OBSOLETE FOOD which induces skepti-
cism, sloth and pessimism . . . it cannot sustain
physical enthusiasm toward women,'" Nick Hannibal read from Marinetti's *Futurist Cuisine,* a
book Molly Rafferty had tossed on a living room table when
she came back from her afternoon class. "Your edition's only
two years old." He paged through the volume scowling and
occasionally snorting. "Is there really a market for proto-fas-
cist writers?"

"No," she said, sitting down next to him, "but there's an
immense boom in cookbooks. I bought it in a smart little
kitchenware shop the last time I was in Milan."

"Did you assign it?" She'd annotated the book heavily.

"Yes, I taught it today in the women's history colloquium.
Too many Scattergood undergraduates are caught up with
the notion that 'the personal is political.' Male dottiness helps
put the nuttier feminist theories in perspective."

"Marinetti's sauce for the gander, I'll say that." He set the
book down and drew her onto his lap. She was wearing a
peach-colored watered-silk kimono also bought in Milan.
"This color," he said, "is particularly nice when you're warm
and pink after a bath."

"And what, darling, did you have for lunch today?"

"My usual"—he glanced at Marinetti—"pomegranates, raw beef, squash blossoms."

"Male squash blossoms?"

"What else?"

"I really should get dressed," she said without conviction. "It's late and I told the Sternbergs we'd drop in on their party after dinner."

"Not yet."

THEY HAD DINNER that evening at a restaurant in Newnham owned by Sal Valenti, a boyhood friend of Nick's father. Sal had watched over their courtship with anxious solicitude and he still strove to make each meal festive. Tonight he surpassed himself with an audacious fettucini: scallops, fresh salmon, smoked salmon, squid, pistachio nuts, sweet peppers, hot peppers, green onions, red onions. Molly still hadn't managed to identify all its elements when Sal offered seconds.

"Thank you," she said, "this will be more than enough for me, but it's the best I've ever eaten."

"A little more pasta for you, Nick?" Sal urged.

"What do you say?" Nick asked Molly.

"It's up to you. I trust your judgment above any man's."

"I'll risk it. Marinetti and his crowd were wrong about so much."

"Speaking of half-witted thugs," she said. "What did you find out about Tommy Franchetti?"

"He's been doing very well. He hasn't been arrested or even held in protective custody for months. I checked in town and with the Newnham police and the DA's office. It's the longest he's been out of trouble for years."

"You told Margaret?"

"Yes, I called her this morning with the good news and with a piece of gossip I heard at the Limerick Bar."

Molly looked at him questioningly.

"The night you took Margaret out to Scattergood to see the multimedia tribute to Frances Perkins . . ."

"It wasn't half bad. It's the senior honors project of a girl with a dual major in history and film studies."

"I'm sure it was inspiring. But I was listening to the voice of the people elsewhere and I heard that Franchetti has a new girlfriend."

"Do you think he's monogamous?"

"I haven't any idea, but it's thought to be the first sustained interest he's shown in anyone since Donna left him."

"YOU'LL LIKE LLEWELLYN," she said as they drove to the Sternbergs'. "I'm dying to know whether Sam has actually convinced the gang at the Center to make him an offer."

"He works on populism, you said. Did you get to his talk?"

"Yes, and it was terrific. He's studied generations of farm families and developed some really marvelous notions about who does and who doesn't shift from left to right. It's been done on the level of biography before—a reformer begins attacking banks and railroads and ends up hallucinating about Jews and blacks—but never on the scale Llewellyn's attempting."

"It doesn't sound like the sort of work the Center's famous for."

"That's the problem. Sam's near despair at the shallow trendiness of the place. Miranda wouldn't be entertaining these people if something important wasn't at stake. She hasn't spoken to Norman Clawsen or to Bert Harding since they dropped the course on genocide."

"Why did they do that?"

"Harding said Marvell shouldn't have 'ghetto' courses."

"YOU'VE JUST MISSED DICK LLEWELLYN," Miranda Sternberg greeted them at the door. She was an artless, handsome woman who wore no makeup and little jewelry except her wedding ring and an odd pre-Columbian bauble she'd been meaning to give to a museum but which so resembled a favorite garter snake or the frog in the garden pond that her children begged her to keep it for a while. "George Gresham's still here though, pressing the flesh like a young Lyndon Johnson," she said, after taking them upstairs to see the children and down again to the threshold of the living room, thronged with chattering Marvellites, where she left them.

"Which one is Bertram Harding?" Nick asked Molly.

"The epicene one with the dagger in his belt. Don't you recognize him?"

"He looks a little different from his pictures," Nick said. "Where did he get that dagger?"

"In one of the Trucial States. Miranda told me he's consulting on a new constitution for an emirate."

"I've read him on police brutality. He thinks it's a good thing."

"You know about academics," she said. "They admire what they lack. Harding exemplifies the *on admire ce qu'on manque* school of political science. Take an outrage and he finds a bright side, so long as someone is beating up somebody or making money doing it." They'd seen little of each other in recent days, so they tarried in conversation, enjoying the perfect privacy large parties afford. Their hostess had plunged into the crowd, determined to talk with Audrey Clawsen.

"I got the impression from Harding's work on law enforce-

ment that there's more to his method than vicarious fun,"
Nick said. "He seems to survey a topic, take a position a little
to the right of the scholarly consensus, and then peddle his
conclusions as realism."

"He's done that a number of times. He finds some practice,
the more opprobrious the better, and announces that it has
hitherto unacknowledged social utility. Naturally, the people
who've been doing it all along—reaping most of the suppos-
edly hidden benefits—are plenty grateful to Bert for their
newfound respectability. He *was* ingenious about corporate
tax evasion," Molly had to admit.

"What's the social utility there?" Nick asked, taking two
glasses of champagne from the waiter who insinuated himself
between them.

"Form of disguised saving," she explained.

"What's he finding functional in the emirate? Slavery?"

"No, he calls it 'educative autocracy.' "

"Colonialists used to say 'tutelage.' " Nick sipped the
Sternbergs' excellent champagne.

"And they often went about it more responsibly. Bert
claims he can identify forms of repression ultimately condu-
cive to democracy."

"Must call for some nice distinctions."

"All his activities in the Middle East require nice distinctions. He's on several sides of everything, trying to be even-
handed."

"Even-handed, but not empty-handed. That's a fine dagger. Who's the man talking with him?"

"Norman Clawsen. He's an Americanist. He pretty well
has to be because it's the only language he can both speak
and read. I don't think he writes in any human tongue.
Come, I'll introduce you."

"Bert," Norman Clawsen was saying as Nick and Molly
made their way toward them, "have you ever mentioned my

Crisis Situation Simulation workbook to the emir? I'm sure he could utilize it to update his infrastructure."

"Sorry, pal," Harding replied, draining his glass and reaching for another wedge of brie baked in phyllo. "The emir ain't got an infrastructure. All he's got is vassals. They're bedouins, for God's sake."

Alvin Worth reached Clawsen and Harding before Nick and Molly did. "I am sure we could adapt the workbook to his needs," he said. "I'm contributing the ethics modules and I've worked up several based on Islamic principles. It would not do, Norman, to approach a deeply religious man like the emir with merely secular expertise."

"Forget it, guys," Harding said, scooping up a handful of macadamia nuts. "Nobody in Al Awash could read your workbook. Hell, the grand vizier's the only one of them who knows any English at all, and his TOEFL's only three-twenty."

"How do you know the vizier's TOEFL score?" Worth asked.

"What *is* a TOEFL?" Clawsen had never heard of it.

"Test of English as a Foreign Language," Harding explained. "They want to send the prince to Groton and the vizier took the test for him, only he didn't do so hot. I took it myself this time. That oughta get the kid in, don'tcha think? I may be a cracker, but I'm a cracker with a Ph.D." He cut himself another hunk of brie. "Why, here's that cute little redhead, Molly Rafferty. Molly, honey, where you been hiding yourself? Scattergood College, right? Hell, that's great. Say, Al, if Molly's at Scattergood, she's not covered by GUPO?"

"Hello, Bert," Molly said. "I'm still at Scattergood and this is my fiancé, Nick Hannibal."

"Hiyah"—Harding enveloped her in a clumsy hug and extended a hand to Nick—"and congratulations. You're a lucky fella. Molly's real sweet, for such a brainy little lady."

"Thank you," Nick said.

"You all know my colleagues, Norman Clawsen and Alvin Worth?"

"What's this GUPO that doesn't include Molly?" Nick asked after shaking hands with Clawsen and Worth.

"I defer to you, Alvin," Clawsen said.

"GUPO has become an acronym for some principles I outlined to help clarify the Center's policy on the distressing problem of improper, uh, inappropriate relations between the sexes."

"Has sexual harassment been a problem at Marvell?" Molly wondered if anyone would be frank.

"Not at the Center, happily," Clawsen answered. "No doubt in part because of our timely preemptive measures. Al's guidelines governing unprofessional overtures are very complete."

"But they don't cover other institutions," Harding roared. "How 'bout that, Molly. You're fair game at Scattergood, but you turn up as good as married. What do you do, Nick?"

"I'm a policeman."

"Commissioner's a friend of mine," Harding said.

"Yes, he often refers to your work." At the commissioner's request, Nick lectured police recruits several times each year on the inadequacy of Harding's theories.

"That's great. You got a specialty?"

"Homicide."

"Hot dog," Harding said. "Rank?"

"Lieutenant."

"Damn, that's fine. Let's go find a real drink. Say, Nick, you ought to keep this little girl safe at home. Sexual harassment's a real serious problem. I wouldn't want my wife hassled by a bunch of randy nerds."

Nick was tempted to give Harding practical experience of police brutality, but Molly spoke up quickly. "I know you'd like a chance to talk with Bert, Nick. And I want to hear about the candidates for the American politics job."

"Richard Llewellyn had, evidently, some more pressing engagement," Alvin Worth told her. "George Gresham is here, I'm happy to say, and you will be able to form your own opinion of him."

Worth propelled Molly through the crowd to the spot where Gresham, abandoned by Emory Stokes, stood alone. The young Texan had, Molly saw, an insufficiently nuanced view of the Eastern establishment. He had dressed for this austere and high-minded crowd in an extremity of Manhattan modishness. A good tailor would have found his figure challenging, but an expensive ready-made jacket revealed his shoulders to be as unstructured as the garment itself. This slope of dull-olive silk gabardine was surmounted by the small pale face, weak white-lashed eyes and tow-colored hair of the near-albino backwoodsman.

Worth performed the introduction, then hurried away, intent on bringing Miranda Sternberg into the conversation.

"Molly Rafferty," Gresham said. "That's your name?" He had never heard of her.

"Yes, it is."

"Don't you use your husband's name?" Who was she?

"I expect I will after I'm married."

"Oh, you're getting married. What field is he in?"

"Law enforcement."

"At Marvell?" Gresham asked.

"No."

"Are you at Marvell?"

"No."

"Gee, it's been great to meet you," he said, and moved on.

Worth, who had been unable to find Miranda, caught up with Gresham minutes later. "Where is Molly Rafferty?"

Gresham's mouth was full and Worth repeated his question impatiently, adding that Molly Rafferty was, unaccountably, very highly regarded by both Sternbergs and that her support would be helpful to him. "She was involved a few years ago with an old and intimate friend of theirs and when he jilted her they cut him dead."

Primed about Molly's importance and her field, and desperate to avoid the other man's fate, Gresham sought her out. "I believe in quantification," he told her. "It's essential in history too."

"Of course," she agreed, "for things that can be counted or measured, but there are lots of things that can't be. A style or a period, something that's readily grasped, you can characterize it, interpret it, sympathize with it, but it doesn't make sense to quantify . . ."

He interrupted her with an incomprehensible account of his research, which he felt made his point.

"I do understand the impulse," she said. " 'In measurement began our might' and all that."

"Say, that's good. I haven't read much theory. Is it Kenneth Arrow's?"

"What?"

" 'In measurement began our might,' " he repeated.

"It's Yeats," she said.

"Where is he?"

"He's dead."

Nick Hannibal joined them. A hard-drinking senator, whose company Bert Harding preferred even to a cop's, had just arrived. "George has been telling me about his thesis. He believes that political ideas must be tested empirically."

"So do I," Nick said and wished Gresham luck with his research. "I'll get our coats."

Gresham set off to meet the senator. Worth and Clawsen had been standing by, monitoring Gresham's appeal, and they stepped in to explain Llewellyn's shortcomings to Molly, who remained obtuse to their objections. "In any case," Clawsen concluded, "Llewellyn's work has all been done before. Wretched people unable to cope with modern life. It's nothing new."

"What more could anyone find to say about *ressentiment?*" Worth asked with distaste.

"Lots," Molly protested. "Themes like resentment and revenge can never be exhausted."

"You really do not understand," Clawsen said. "Historical interpretation doesn't settle anything. Political science has immeasurably, or indeed I should say measurably, progressed . . ."

"Since Thucydides?" Nick Hannibal asked. He was carrying their coats, but this conversation was too good to cut short.

Clawsen, who was indefatigable, attempted to enlighten him. A masculine intelligence, he thought, might prove less stubbornly irrational than Molly's. It was essential, he explained, to formulate a hypothesis that could be either confirmed or refuted, then to find or contrive situations that tested the thesis. This, he said, was called "operationalizing the insight." Lastly, one must accumulate a sufficient *n,* that was to say, a number of examples that definitively established the truth or the falsity of the proposition.

"It's been a pleasure talking with you," Nick said to Clawsen when he really did not want to hear any more and Molly had for some minutes been signaling her impatience. "You've encouraged me to test a political proposition."

"Be sure it's one you can operationalize," Clawsen advised earnestly. "That step is often the most difficult of all."

"I'll think of something." Nick, helping Molly with her coat, spoke softly into her ear. "I want to refute Marinetti's hypothesis about the emasculating effects of pasta."

*　*　*

"WHAT GIGGLES ARE YOU stifling in your pillow?" he asked early the next morning.

"I thought you were asleep," she turned over and laughed aloud. "The n, how great would the n have to be?"

"Molly, you astonish me."

"What *would* suffice to refute Marinetti?" she challenged him. "Shouldn't the n be greater?"

"I'd spare no pains to discredit him."

"That's what I hoped you'd say."

EIGHT

THE SEARCH COMMITTEE REMAINED DIVIDED, though more and more people at Marvell were saying they thought Llewellyn brilliant. Clawsen couldn't see it himself, but he did see—and he resented—the pleasure the young man took in his work. George Gresham had attended his rival's talk and done himself no good. Llewellyn called on him in the question and answer session with mannerly promptness; doubtless because, Alvin Worth pointed out afterward, he expected Gresham to shoot himself in the foot. George had, indeed, raised some sweaty quibble that Llewellyn easily resolved. It was worrying. Last night at the Sternbergs' party, with Llewellyn unaccountably absent, George might have handled himself better. He'd taken to wearing a Marvell College tie too. Only real Marvell men, current and former undergraduates, properly wore the tie. Others who assumed that prerogative were taken for tourists, or worse. They must tell him to stop.

As Clawsen trudged through the grimy slush from the Center to the subway station, rain pelting derisively down laid bare the dirt beneath the snow. It was December 15, his wedding anniversary, and Audrey had taken the car to be inspected. The car's sticker was good until the end of the month, but Audrey was piqued because when she'd asked him that morning if he remembered what day it was, he'd said that it was time to have the car inspected.

"Right, absolutely right." She'd risen from the breakfast table, her grapefruit untouched. "I shouldn't put it off any longer." She'd snatched her car coat from the peg on the kitchen wall. "The lights may not pass," she'd called from the hall as she left. "I'll have to keep the car all day. You'll have to take the bus."

Audrey knew he hated public transportation as much as he loved his reserved parking place at the Center, although he could easily get home by subway and bus: the trip took less than forty minutes. Unable to afford the real country, the Clawsens lived not very far out of Boston in a town where spuriously colonial houses stood close together on streets with revolutionary names. They were at the end of Paine Drive where it met Pursuit of Happiness Way curving into a *cul-de-sac.*

Clawsen loathed the descent into the subway station and loathed the hot crowded cars. Two boys were tracing obscenities with their hockey sticks on the steamy windows of the car he dejectedly entered. He squeezed into a seat and, in an effort to keep up with recent scholarship, took a journal from his briefcase.

The hockey players' raucousness distracted him, the more so because he recognized one of them as a local high school star hotly recruited that fall by Marvell. The boy did not utter three consecutive words unpunctuated by filthy expletives in the course of the ride. Clawsen feared he'd be seeing more of him because half the hockey team generally majored in political science. The coach had already traipsed this lout through the Center, hoping to dazzle him with Marvell's stars. Clawsen stared fixedly at the printed page until the train stopped.

The subway line ended in a prizewinning terminus, honored for architectural inventiveness as well as a high degree of community involvement in its planning and design. Built with vaulting pipes and soaring crystal shafts, the suburban bus station was a masterpiece of high-tech Gothic. It was Gothic, too, in its marriage of city and country, exaltation and whimsy. Naive decorations, strewn lavishly about, curbed its loftiness, and the clay-colored floor of its central hall spawned wild creatures: bronze field mice, frogs, sparrowhawks, snails, rabbits, chipmunks, and coiling snakes, all pressed in vigorous intaglio, had been scattered among its earth-brown floor tiles.

Clawsen stepped thoughtlessly on one of the bullfrogs. He ground his foot on it and wished as he resumed his walk, going out of his way now to tread on wild things, that he could crush them all underfoot: the toady Stokes; the coiled, supple snakes—Llewellyn, a young snake, lithe and effortlessly clever, Sam Sternberg, an older cannier snake, wise with an ageless malevolence; the dean, Caleb Tuttle, whose aged head with its hard, glittering eyes rose tortoise-like on a long wrinkled neck; and Harding. Yes, Harding was there, too, the unspeakable Harding, a fat jackrabbit hopping around the world copulating. Clawsen spared the snails. These seemed to him as self-effacing as his friend Alvin Worth: the snails would not stick their necks out, but they kept their antennae poised. They were soft though, soft and squishy inside.

He tramped methodically across the hall, grinding his enemies beneath his heel. A few people noticed his progress and wondered if he needed help. When he reached the escalator, he grasped its handrail as if it were a lifeline towing him out of a swamp. Not for a moment did he consider taking the elevator instead. He would not encase himself in that crystal cage; he would not hang there exposed.

Clawsen made his way to the bus platforms, exposed but not so starkly open as the glass elevators. Glass-paneled stainless steel doors opened on three sides to the bays where the buses idled. On the fourth side, a wall was decorated, in a flight of fancy surprising in a public building, with a *trompe l'oeil* mural. Clawsen sank, heavily for one so slender, onto a bench and gazed at the dappled pasture painted on the south wall, glimpsed seemingly through a fourth set of glass and metal doors. Cows, richly ruminant, lay on flower-strewn grass. One animal stood watching the commuters as they kept their joyless appointments, incredulous that anyone would forsake the meadow where she and her sisters eternally browsed. The boldest of the herd poked her nose, a brown velvet muzzle wet with dew, through the open door. Clawsen longed for that rural, that irrecoverable past.

"I'm a farm boy myself," he said, "goddammit, a farm boy." He was glad, as he boarded his bus, to see that the rain had changed to snow.

MARGARET DONAHUE, sitting alone at a long table in the Center's library, looked up from her work and saw a couple walking hand in hand through the snow, pausing now and then to kiss. She supposed it was a sign of her age that she was beginning to notice again things she had put resolutely from her mind years before. Margaret had not determined to remain unmarried, but she had never, after breaking up nastily with one man, cared deeply about another. As a high school teacher she daily witnessed the most graceless sexual display. A day spent among flaunting, simpering, groping adolescents, she thought, could sour you on sex for a long time. Yet recently she had found herself imagining that honest feelings might prompt even their inept and ostentatious fondling. This couple, however, was not inept. They embraced, picture-perfect, under a streetlamp, like a couple in a paperweight, with snow swirling around them, falling like blossoms on the girl's dark hair.

She watched them benignly and then, to her surprise, recognized them: Dick Llewellyn, whose talk had been even better than his articles, and Donna Franchetti. Margaret was startled to see them together, although their first meeting had been memorable. They would be waiting at that corner, she supposed, because it was Donna's bus stop. A few minutes later, Dick boarded the bus with Donna; as it pulled away from the curb, Tom Franchetti emerged from a side street and stalked after it.

"Hi, Margaret." Jake Larson sat down across from her. "You still prioritizing or have you moved on to the decision tree?"

"Are you finished already?" she asked. Midcareer fellows were, as part of their curriculum's celebrated realism, confronted from time to time with instructive crises for which they had to devise solutions by nine the next morning. Norman Clawsen, it was rumored, hoped to market a workbook based on these assignments. Alvin Worth had designed accompanying ethics modules, but his exercises were optional for the fellows.

"I haven't even started," Larson said. "Some Teamsters broke up an organizational meeting at a new GM plant in Kentucky and I've just gotten off the phone with the local paper. I want them to get the paramedics' story in print before they're persuaded to forget what they saw."

"How badly were people hurt?"

"Broken bones. No skull injuries for a change. I'll have to go down this weekend."

"Then you won't stay up to do this assignment, will you? Save your energy for a real crisis."

Larson said he'd take a crack at this one. Was it as crazy as the others?

"Asinine," she said. "Listen to this. 'The EPA has discovered that a carcinogenic contaminent has been seeping from a chemical plant into a neighboring marsh for at least twenty years. Leukemia rates are 12.8 percent above the national average, and there is an as-yet-unreleased study of birth defects and infertility in the area. The Defense Department wants to drain the marsh for an airbase, employing two thousand locals but putting an additional strain on existing county services. A private developer wants to build a shopping mall expected to employ upward of three thousand people. He will absorb some but not all of the cleanup costs, but he refuses to detoxify more than three feet below the proposed parking lot area, more than ten feet below the proposed commercial facilities areas, or more than twenty feet below the proposed dining and amenities areas.' " Margaret paused for breath.

"When will the second train get to St. Louis?"

Margaret laughed and read through another page of conflicting constraints and specifications. "And wait until you hear what's omitted."

"Is the governor in your party or the other and is he running for president?"

"Right. Also, who's up for re-election, whether the plant is unionized or not and whether it's privately or publicly held. The assignment is to 'frame the question' for the Secretary of the Interior."

"If you want the swamp drained," Larson suggested, "it might be simpler to frame the Secretary."

"Let's work on a scenario for that and skip the calculations."

They worked steadily, sketching an elaborate sting, until they were interrupted by the return of Richard Llewellyn. He could not have tarried more than a few minutes with Donna in Newnham, Margaret reckoned as the young man wandered into the library, and been back within the hour. She was enormously relieved to see him. Donna was a capable young woman, a consenting adult and all the rest, but Margaret would have been shocked to learn she was spending the night with a man she hardly knew. Moreover, considerations of delicacy aside, Margaret did not trust Tommy Franchetti.

"Been out in the snow?" Larson asked. The elevators that went up to the guest suites stood opposite the entrance to the library. Llewellyn seemed scarcely to know where he was. "It looks like a beautiful night."

"It is a beautiful night," Llewellyn answered, ruddy and elated. "I was taking Donna home." He remembered their solicitude for the young woman. "We had dinner and talked so long afterward that I didn't want her to go home alone."

Margaret nodded her approval.

"Well, good night. Don't work too hard. Take care. It's a great snowstorm." He walked dazedly out of the library past the elevators and bounded up the stairs.

"Donna's very pretty," Larson said.

"And intelligent and responsible. Her estranged husband, on the other hand, as you've seen, is unwilling to divorce her, stupid and vicious."

"Dick Llewellyn looks like he can take care of himself."

"In a fair fight, no doubt he could," Margaret replied grimly. "Are we about finished with the Secretary of the Interior?"

"I think so." Larson got up and peered out the window. "Looks like the snow's sticking. You won't try to make it home tonight, will you?"

"No, I'll stay here and hand in the paper in the morning."

"Then I'll see you at breakfast bright and early. Sleep well."

Margaret signed into one of the guest rooms, kept ready for fellows who chose to spend the night after dinner meetings or late assignments, and drew a bath. She could never fall asleep after writing something; instead she lay awake, rethinking or rephrasing the piece or toying with other approaches to a solution. Tonight her thoughts did not revolve around Professor Clawsen's simulated crises, but around the impending ones she feared. She was worried about Donna and Dick Llewellyn. Nick Hannibal had, as he'd promised, looked into Tommy Franchetti's recent comings and goings and his report had been reassuring. Margaret fretted, although she recognized as she lay back in the steaming water that she shouldn't. Nick Hannibal was tough-minded and dependable. Donna was level-headed, and Larson was doubtless right: Llewellyn could handle Franchetti.

But could Jake himself handle the Teamsters? Margaret was a woman capable of deep and sustained indignation, and nothing enraged her more than hoodlumism in organized labor. It had been a mistake, she remained convinced, to readmit the Teamsters into the AFL-CIO. They were pretty tame in Massachusetts, but she did not trust them, individually or collectively. Larson struck her as a good and decent man, wry, unassuming, sensible. The more she thought about it, the more distressed she became.

She slept fitfully and next morning asked Larson without preliminaries when he was leaving for Kentucky.

He told her he was going down that night and returning Sunday evening. "Organizing's in an early stage," he continued. "I don't expect serious trouble, but I'll call you if I need reinforcements."

"You could call anyway," she said, "to say you're in one piece. I'll feel better about you being down there if you check back with me."

"Okay, I will. Around six on Saturday?"

"Don't forget."

NINE

"I FIND LLEWELLYN, how shall I put it," Alvin Worth simpered, "belletristic." The search committee, professors and midcareer fellows, were gathered one last time before they scattered for the winter vacation to thrash out their differences over George Gresham and Richard Llewellyn. Worth was holding Xandu Tikibinitantari, the Thai prodigy, in reserve as a bargaining chip. "Yes," he sighed, "belletristic."

"What does that mean?" Lou Stillman, the fellow from the International Ladies Garment Workers Union, often asked awkward questions. Stillman was about sixty—Worth had checked his application—plump, white-haired and mildly rumpled; he wore oddly matched clothing as if he regarded the fashion industry as the enemy.

"It means he doesn't use 'access' or 'dialogue' as verbs," Sam Sternberg said.

"Considerations of style quite apart," Clawsen interrupted, "there are very, very serious objections to his work."

"What are your reservations, Norman?" Caleb Tuttle asked. Sam had suggested he not miss this meeting. "We're relying on you to keep us on the cutting edge."

"You know—that is, I have already expressed my fears—that Llewellyn's work is, methodologically speaking, built on sand. And that might suffice to exclude him from serious consideration. But even if we judge him as a historian, and overlook his incapability to conduct a political-scientific inquiry—he has not done his homework. He does not appear to have read, at any rate nowhere does he cite, Halworthy's pioneering work on the junkets taken by the fifty-fourth Congress, whose members would, as you all know, have been up for re-election in 1896, a year Llewellyn professes to regard as critical."

"And how might Halworthy's findings have informed Llewellyn's work?" Tuttle asked intently. Only Sam Sternberg caught the instantly quelled twitch in the corner of his mouth. Fifteen years of marriage had not diminished the awe he felt for Brahmin civility. His wife, too, was enchanting with people whom she particularly disliked, though he feared her party hadn't much advanced Llewellyn's cause.

"I would not presume to say," Clawsen replied, "but it is the *minimal* expectation one would have for a first-year graduate student, let alone a junior colleague, that he, he or she," he corrected himself, "would survey all the secondary literature."

"Even if it's drivel?" Sternberg asked. He understood and valued civility himself, but he was beginning to feel the time had come for plain speaking. He was about to call for a straw vote when Lou Stillman threw up his hands, a parody of exasperation.

"Oh, you *yeshiva bokkers!*" Stillman exclaimed. "Llewellyn is a smart young man, sharp as a tack. Heart in the right place too. And there's some text he didn't mention? That's the trouble, isn't it, Sammy? Some obscure text?" Sternberg nodded. "So what does it matter? You shouldn't be such a stickler, Professor Clawsen. No offense, but here you are a famous professor and you're still behaving like a *yeshiva bokker.*"

In the stunned silence that followed, the dean did raise his eyebrows, and Sam Sternberg, although, like his wife, he hated to see people discomfited, did not say, as he so easily might have, "Norm wouldn't know what a *yeshiva bokker* is, Lou, he's a Midwesterner." Sternberg was far too curious to hear what Clawsen himself would say.

"That expression is unfamiliar to me," Clawsen replied, after a long struggle to master his rage. "I take it that it means something akin to pedant."

"Yes," Stillman explained, "a little too scrupulous about details. Not that respect for learning isn't a good thing, reverence for it even, but sometimes, you know, you can miss the main point."

Margaret Donahue hurried to Llewellyn's defense. She thought it unlikely that anything Stillman could say would mollify Clawsen, whose throat and jaw remained contorted with fury. "But that's exactly what I like so much about Llewellyn's work. He uses such a variety of sources. It seems to me he's dug up remarkable evidence. He's looked up the WPA oral histories of the whole region and gone back through the unpublished interviews that went into preparing them."

"WPA histories—" Clawsen, given a subject upon which he could vent his wrath, was now positively shrieking. "Unpublished interviews conducted by amateurs. WPA oral histories from the Depression. The most revolting Populist sentimentality. You might as well try to learn about the Midwest from, from . . ."

"Sinclair Lewis?" Jake Larson proposed. He was doodling and did not look up from his notebook.

"Yes," Clawsen hiccupped his gratitude and resumed his tirade. "Miss Donahue, you cannot possibly be conversant with these pretended histories. They are," he attempted gallantry, "before your time."

"They are not," she said.

"Well, then"—his wan smile became a more ghastly leer—

"you look much younger than you are." Margaret loathed being told she looked younger than she was. It was so blatant a lie. "But," Clawsen continued, oblivious to her anger, "let me assure you that we in political science are light years away from that sorry time."

"The New Deal was a bad time," Lou Stillman said, "and this is a good one? You could have fooled me."

"Light years away. We have made great strides in political science since then," Clawsen gasped. *"Where* are Harding and Stokes?" He looked at the door to see if it would open and admit help.

"On their way," Worth said, passing him a note that read, "Stokes hung over. Suspect Bert violating GUPO."

"I've read some of the WPA studies myself," Larson ventured to say, although Clawsen evidently thought the subject closed.

"Many of them?" Clawsen asked, more calmly.

"A few. They were interesting. These interviewers found, among other things, that some families had been suspicious of banks for generations. In the Depression, people drew on memories of the 1890s."

"That's right," Margaret said. "Llewellyn told me it made a big difference if people recognized the arguments demagogues like Father Coughlin were making, if they'd heard them before from people they trusted."

"I suppose," Tuttle said, "that's what Llewellyn means by the resonance of an idea." He'd been offering the mildest of comments, taking care not to preempt the chairman's role.

"Moreover," Stillman saw another possibility, "it would have mattered for Roosevelt's campaigns what voters thought . . . about banks, about corporations . . ."

"I bet it mattered a lot," Sam Sternberg reflected. "Critics of the WPA always charged that its interviewers proselytized, but I imagine what they heard about the way people were thinking proved much more useful than anything they said themselves."

"I don't doubt that," Larson agreed. "It cuts organizing time in half if you understand people's preconceptions." He'd spent a productive weekend in Kentucky largely because UAW organizers had done their homework.

"That's right." Tuttle had learned a considerable amount of Slavic folklore early in 1942.

"But they were not scientific." Clawsen could stand it no longer.

"Gentlemen," Worth said. He thought Clawsen might be having a stroke. "We cannot act without Bert and Emory. Let's break now and reconvene in an hour . . . and Ms. Donahue, of course." He regretted saying "gentlemen," really he should have learned by now. He laid a hand on Clawsen's wrist casually and felt for a pulse. Rapid, he thought, but not dangerously so.

"An excellent idea, Al," Tuttle said. The committee was rising from the seminar table when Harding burst through the door, struggling out of his vicuña overcoat.

"Was your plane late again, Bert?" Worth asked.

"Nope, I was on the phone at home. Buzz called from the White House while I was in the shower and there I was, naked as a jaybird, talking to the Secretary and dripping on the bath mat." He looked around the room at his colleagues, who seemed to be dispersing. "You haven't wrapped it up without me?" he asked, surprised unanimity had been so speedily reached. "I've got a line on a kid who'll knock your socks off."

"We'd just decided to wait for you and Emory, Bert," Tuttle said. "We'll meet back here in an hour and you can tell us about your candidate then."

Harding followed Worth and Clawsen to Worth's office, where Clawsen lowered himself into a reclining chair. "You don't look so good, Norm," Harding said, not unkindly.

"I think he's coming down with the flu," Worth said. "I'll stay with him. Would you ask the kitchen to send up a pot of tea?"

"Okay," Harding said. "I'll be in the library."

"I want to talk to you about that," Worth said, stepping into the corridor. "Are you aware that the young woman Donna Franchetti is covered by GUPO?"

"Like hell she is," Harding retorted. "She's a librarian. She's not a student or a junior colleague. I don't grade her, write recommendations for her, hire, fire, or promote her."

"She is enrolled in courses." Worth smiled.

"Not in my courses."

"It doesn't matter. GUPO explicitly prohibits relationships whenever there is any asymmetry of position."

"I'll stick to the missionary position." Harding chuckled.

"I thought I should remind you of our guidelines, but you may not get the opportunity to assume any position with that particular young woman. I saw Llewellyn bidding her a prolonged farewell in the library this morning. Perhaps he dropped by on his way to the airport. Or perhaps he accompanied her to work. I couldn't say."

"ALVIN," NORMAN CLAWSEN ASKED, as his friend reentered his office with a tea tray, "how could that devious young twerp Llewellyn have known the Donahue woman was interested in Father Coughlin and the WPA?"

"I haven't any idea. But it's all in his manuscript, so it's not surprising they talked about it. Drink this, Norman, you really look ill."

"In the manuscript, you say?"

"Norman, haven't you read his submissions?" Worth was genuinely appalled.

"Not every word. How could I? It's such junk!"

*   *   *

A MORE CONVIVIAL PARTY drank coffee and ate bagels and muffins in the Center's cafeteria. "I'm sorry I upset Professor Clawsen," Lou Stillman was saying. "I know it's wrong to use foreign expressions other people don't understand."

"Like belletristic," Margaret Donahue laughed. "In fairness, I don't think Yiddish is any less familiar to most people here than French."

"But I was sure he was Jewish," Stillman said. "You could have fooled me."

"No," Sam explained, "that was the problem. He couldn't fool you."

"And everything Dick Llewellyn wrote about Father Coughlin rings true," Margaret said. "My father painted him in the thirties."

"His portrait?" Lou Stillman asked, askance. He liked Margaret and she'd struck him as more the Dorothy Day sort of Catholic.

"Certainly not his portrait. He painted him as a snake oil salesman in a WPA mural in Newnham's main post office."

"Gutsy," Jake said. "Coughlin must have been pretty popular in a city like yours."

"Dad was a gutsy guy," Margaret remembered his fervor. "He thought art should educate the people."

THE SEARCH COMMITTEE AGREED, when it reassembled, that it was far from consensus. Sternberg and the fellows wanted Llewellyn, but agreed to see Harding's dark horse. Clawsen and Worth declared themselves for Gresham, unalterably opposed to Llewellyn and willing, if the others were, to entertain new applications. Stokes, if he turned up, would side

with one or the other of his richer and better known colleagues. No one knew whether he'd plunk for Sternberg's
favorite or Harding's. The dean, reticent in meetings, said
nothing, but Gresham's backers were sure he'd advance
Llewellyn's candidacy among the many, many people at Marvell who venerated him.

Caleb Tuttle, however, was about to go on leave. He'd be
in Eastern Europe most of the spring, and in more than
usually out-of-the-way places. In consequence, Alvin Worth
announced that he'd learned only yesterday that an exceptionally brilliant graduate student, not hitherto on the job
market for the coming fall, would be completing his dissertation ahead of schedule. He was a twenty-year-old In-
dochinese refugee whose paper had brought the political science profession to its feet in a standing ovation at the
previous summer's convention.

"What's his name?" Sam Sternberg asked. A professor of
law, he was not obliged to parley with political scientists.

"Tikibinitantari."

"Sounds Thai," Sam said.

"Yes, I believe he is an ethnic Thai, but I understand his
family were shopkeepers in Cambodia and that he is the sole
survivor of a Khmer Rouge massacre," Worth lied, knowing it
to be a lie several of the others must, at least provisionally,
accept. Tikibinitantari was, in truth, the *idiot savant* son of a
rich Bangkok restaurateur, so mortified by the boy's oddity
that he paid an American university handsomely to keep him
not only out of Thailand but out of Asia.

"How terrible," Margaret said.

"And," Worth continued, "now that his student days are
drawing to a close, there may be some problem about his
visa."

"If it's a case for asylum, we must see him," Sam said.

"There'll be no difficulty with extending his visa," Caleb
Tuttle promised authoritatively.

They agreed to hear Tikibinitantari early in January and to lunch once more with Gresham and Llewellyn, separately.

"How soon can we do that?" Harding asked.

"George is in Boston for the vacation," Clawsen said. "He has an aunt somewhere on the South Shore."

"And I overheard Llewellyn say he would be back before New Year's, Bert." Worth contributed this item wickedly. "He *said* he wanted to look at nineteenth-century colored lithographs in the Boston Public Library, but perhaps he just likes the city."

"Swell," Harding said. "The sooner the better. And I'll get my girl up here just as soon as she's free to come north."

"What do women see in Bert?" Clawsen asked Worth as they retired to the ethicist's office to discuss the meeting.

"Why should you ask me?" Worth was a bachelor and lived alone. He did not prefer men to women; he did not much like either sex, and Harding's unquenchable libido revolted him. "I find his enthusiasm more incomprehensible than his success."

"And what can Llewellyn want with colored lithographs?"

"He purports to be interested in political culture," Worth answered, "whatever that may be. But there's money in art. Don't you remember when Bert brought out that coffee-table book of anti-Tammany cartoons? That netted him a pretty penny."

"I remember. The bastard really has a golden touch. He seduced the graduate student who was cataloging them, promised to make her a coauthor and sold the idea to Random House."

"He told Emory he wrote the introduction on the shuttle going down to New York. He spent more time romancing the girl than writing the text. And he didn't drop her until she'd finished proofreading the galleys." Worth shook his head. "All that happened before GUPO."

"I wish he would drop dead," Clawsen said, with much feeling.

A howl of anguish answered him. Bert Harding ran shrieking down the corridor, not struck dead but sorely afflicted.

"I am not a superstitious man," Worth smiled. "Nonetheless, your words seem to have taken effect almost instantly."

A calamity had befallen Bert Harding. His jeweled dagger was missing, stolen. He kept it in a wall safe in his office, to which he'd returned after the search committee meeting. He was planning to fly down to Washington that evening for a Christmas party at which he was, for several reasons, eager to shine. He'd taken the treasure from his safe and put it in his briefcase, then left his office momentarily. When he got back, he opened the case and took the scabbard out, not, he said, from any uneasiness, but for the pure pleasure of seeing the beautiful thing within.

And then, he told the Center's security guards, the Marvell police who soon joined them and those of his colleagues who remained at the Center on the last afternoon before the winter vacation, he'd found a cheap hunting knife in its place. Police and guards cooperated in a thorough but fruitless hunt for the missing dagger, and the longest night of the year was many hours old before faculty and fellows dispersed into its shadows.

TEN

IT WAS UNFORTUNATE that so few people visited the Boston Public Library on the afternoon of New Year's Eve. Had anyone other than the library's curator of prints found the body slumped over a triumphant series of lithographs executed to celebrate the coming of the railroad to the Dakota Territory, Nick Hannibal's task would have been easier. A custodian, another researcher, any reader of detective fiction would have known not to move the body. But, the curator protested, he had felt for a pulse and found none before he shifted the corpse to rescue the papers beneath. Had it been possible to do anything at all to help the unfortunate victim he would have done that first, naturally. He added, in testy defense of his humanity, that he had telephoned 911 and asked for a doctor before turning his attention to the lithographs, which were already lamentably stained. Perhaps Lieutenant Hannibal was unaware that there existed no other complete set of those prints? There had been one in Henry Ford's museum at Dearborn, but . . .

Hannibal cut short the curator's account of the laxity of private museums and attempted to redirect the man's attention to the body he had disturbed. Hannibal established to his satisfaction that the victim had, most likely, been engrossed in his work and had not turned from it when another person or persons entered the reading room. After he was stabbed, he'd apparently fallen forward onto the library table. But the curator had cleared the table's surface, so it was hard to know what, if anything, the killer had carried away. "Was the victim carrying a briefcase or any papers of his own?" Hannibal asked.

"I don't recollect that he came in with anything but this notebook." The curator handed a standard college-ruled pad to the detective. "He might have checked something downstairs."

"Did he use the library regularly?"

"No, today was his first time, though he may have been familiar with our collection. Our catalog would be on microfiche in any good research library. It is a premier collection of American graphic art."

"Yes." Hannibal saw no reason to dispute the claim. "Do you know who he is or where he's from?"

"Of course. He signed himself him. Visiting scholars must identify themselves. He signed the register." The curator gestured to a book lying open on a table near the door.

Hannibal read the last entry: Richard Llewellyn, History Department, University of Indiana at Bloomington. Then he returned to the body while a police department pathologist completed his preliminary examination.

"Stabbed in the back by someone of at least average strength who is either knowledgeable or lucky. I'll want to look into the wound more thoroughly, but the blade of the knife seems to have sliced through the lung directly into the heart." Nick noticed that a button was missing from Llewellyn's sports jacket; the threads that had secured the button were torn and the wool surrounding them raised as if the button had been tugged rather than fallen off.

After Llewellyn's body was removed, Hannibal had a few more questions for the curator, who said he was not generally alone on Saturday afternoons. He had duties more pressing than monitoring the reading room, but since it was New Year's Eve he had given his staff the afternoon off. He himself wanted to study some prints sent him for his opinion, so he was happy to accommodate the young scholar who had been most appreciative because his time in Boston was short. Llewellyn had arrived at about two o'clock; after chatting briefly with him, the curator retired to his private office, where he worked, uninterrupted and hearing nothing amiss, until about four-fifteen when he went to look for a reference book and found Llewellyn dead.

"The prints you were appraising?" Nick asked. "Were they valuable? Might someone have expected to find you alone?"

"No," the curator replied. "They are historical curiosities. Lincoln drawn in a rather negroid fashion. The owner wanted to know whether they antedated his election or were done around the time of the Emancipation Proclamation. One still turns to Boston with questions like that."

"I'm sure one does." Nick thought he would need most of the night to examine the library, but first he called Molly. "Molly," he began, "there's been a murder at the Boston Public Library. I'm so sorry . . ."

"It's all right. You don't choose your hours." They had planned to go dancing and then come home to spend their first New Year's Eve together quite alone. Molly was making an elegant supper.

"This is unusually bad news, Molly," he said. "It's Richard Llewellyn who's been murdered."

"No. How can that be?" She was silent for a moment. "Are you sure it's the same Richard Llewellyn?"

"Yes, unless there are two of them in the history department at Indiana. He signed into the reading room."

"Do you want me to do anything?"

"No, I'm going to call Sam Sternberg and ask him to identify the body."

"May I tell Margaret? I had lunch with her today. She talked for half an hour about how great Llewellyn was and lent me his dissertation. She said the two other labor fellows on the search committee were tremendously impressed with him too."

"Sure. I think she'd rather hear it from you than from the evening news."

"You don't think anyone else would use Llewellyn's name, do you?" Molly rarely grasped at straws, but she wanted this news to be false. "He's about five ten, wiry, with dark hair and light eyes."

"I'm afraid it's Llewellyn," he said. "I don't know when I'll get home."

He went through the two other rooms on the top floor of the old library building. Another reading room had been closed, and apparently undisturbed, since noon. But the gallery, at the end of the corridor farthest from the Charlotte Cushman Room, where Llewellyn had been working, was open and unattended all day. The photographs on exhibition there were good but not so good they required special precautions against handling or theft; it was impossible to tell if anyone had been in the room.

In one spot where someone might have hidden, a small balcony that opened off the gallery and overhung the courtyard between the old building and the new wing, Hannibal found a small dirty V-shaped piece of snow, compressed as if it might have been embedded in the treads of a heavy shoe and shaken loose, perhaps, when someone stamped his feet to keep warm. The stone floor of the balcony was very cold. It had been cold all week, no more than twenty degrees at noon, so the sliver of snow could have been there for days. Hannibal thought it was worth photographing anyway and had it sent to the lab for analysis.

Then Hannibal returned to the Charlotte Cushman Room, noticing as he walked down the hall that bits of plaster had been struck from the wall in several places. He completed his survey of the reading room and found Llewellyn's missing button some distance from the table at which the murdered man had been working.

Sam Sternberg identified Dick Llewellyn and made a difficult telephone call to his thesis adviser, who offered, after a few minutes of incoherent grief, to break the news to Llewellyn's parents. Then Sam told Nick that the Center remained convulsed and divided by the previous week's sensational crime, the theft of Bert Harding's emerald dagger.

The Marvell police had turned up nothing but a suggestive discrepancy. Bert had told them he'd left his office briefly to go to the men's room, but a custodian thought he'd seen Harding turn left toward the library and not right toward the men's room when he left his office. Bert was raving mad about the theft. He had put off his trip to Washington to supervise the investigation, and he'd scarcely left the Center since discovering his loss. "He asked, by the way," Sam said, "whether you'd be willing to look into it. He said you seemed to know something about crime. Here's his unlisted number, known only to colonels and kings."

"The custodian's trustworthy, I suppose?" Nick asked, taking the card.

"Long-term employee with no grudges that I know about," Sam said. "God, this is terrible. It's been years since we've seen anyone like Llewellyn."

Nick spent the rest of the night at the library and in the morgue, and he wondered as he drove home in the early hours of New Year's Day, past straggling revelers gray as the wintry dawn, whether there might be some connection between the murder and the theft. He was experienced enough to accept coincidence and to know firsthand of some amazing ones. A knife like Harding's could well have made the wound that killed Llewellyn.

He found Molly asleep in an armchair, wrapped in a heavy

plaid shawl. He looked at her with immense satisfaction: Llewellyn's manuscript lay open on her lap. She had, apparently, been keeping a collegial vigil over the dead man's work and he did not want to wake her. He went quietly to the kitchen to look for something to eat and found the refrigerator full of delicious things, but nothing that suggested itself as breakfast. He closed the fridge softly and put the kettle on.

"You're home?" Molly called from the living room.

"Yes. I'm making coffee."

She joined him, her rough shawl still draped about her. He slipped an arm around her waist and felt the silk beneath. "It's a terrible loss," she said.

"His work was very good?"

"Extraordinarily good. Like Richard Cobb at Oxford. More than an historian, almost a medium for his subjects' voices."

They breakfasted on brioche and a melon that had been obscured by bottles of a little known but excellent Italian traminer.

"The melon's not too cold, is it?" she asked. "It was so ripe I had to refrigerate it."

"It couldn't be better. Tell me more about Harding."

"Are you going to have time to look for his dagger? I called Miranda last night to commiserate, and she told me Bert wanted to borrow you from homicide."

"I'll have time," he said. "Could Harding need money? I don't suppose he'd want to sell such an important present, but he might lose it and collect."

"He lives well. I don't think everyone pays him in kind, though his trophies are famous. Did you see his vicuña coat?"

"Yes, he was wearing it when he left the Sternbergs' party with his friend, the senator."

"Bert got the coat from some villainous South American in the days when he was helping us all distinguish between totalitarian governments, which were bad things, and authoritarian ones, which were not such bad things and might, in time, evolve into fine things."

"Not a winner of a dichotomy."

"No, not even in its day. When Bert turned up in the coat, some wag at Marvell said that was the test: the fluffier the vicuña, the more acceptable the regime."

"Harding gets around. I didn't know he dabbled in Latin American politics too."

"He more than dabbles. His first foreign policy book was a tribute to military government in Chile. It wasn't as bad as some. There were American academics who knew the coup was coming and had their books out before Allende's body was cold. It caused him a lot of embarrassment though."

"How so?"

"A parody of the book appeared in a college newspaper. Hemingwayesque, you can imagine . . . Blood and sun and the virile joys of slaughter . . . Some daily papers picked it up and it eventually ran as an op-ed piece in the *Washington Post.* Harding, who'd been angling for a job with Carter, was laughed out of serious consideration. It took almost a decade for his reputation to recover."

"Well, he seems resilient. I'm going to have a shower and go to bed. It's a little early on New Year's morning to call Harding, even with an offer of help."

"I want to finish Llewellyn's thesis," she said. "I'll join you later."

Nick, emerging from a long shower, had a sudden thought. "Molly, any sign that Llewellyn had a sense of humor?"

"He had everything."

"How old was he in 1976?"

She found his *vita,* which Margaret Donahue had tucked inside the thesis binder. "Nineteen," she said. "Oh, my God. And, after college, he spent four years in the Peace Corps in Peru."

*   *   *

NICK CALLED BERT HARDING early that afternoon and was invited to come out and confer on the case. Harding, wearing a houndstooth jacket, jodhpurs and riding boots, met him under the *porte cocherè* of his impressive house and suggested they walk the grounds.

"When did you last see the dagger?" Nick asked.

"I told the Marvell police," Harding said, "but, of course, you haven't read their report yet. I'll have them send you a copy. I took it out of my safe minutes before I discovered it was gone."

"But did you actually see it when you took it out of the safe?"

"No. I didn't take it out of its sheath when I put it in my briefcase, but I could feel the weight of the blade."

"The hunting knife isn't much lighter, is it? Someone could have switched them earlier."

"Well, sure, hypothetically. But if somebody wanted to make me look like a fool in Washington, what does it matter when he did it?"

"It might matter. When's the last time you're positive you had it?"

"I showed it to a member of the Armed Services Committee who was visiting the Center the previous day, the day before I was supposed to go to Washington. I may have forgotten to lock my office when I went to lunch with him. I did leave my office for a spell after I packed up my briefcase." They were walking through an apple orchard, and Harding stopped from time to time to check if a tree had been properly pruned in the fall or would require attention next spring.

"And how long's a spell?" Nick was curious to see how Harding would handle the discrepancy between his own account and his colleagues' version.

"Longer than I made out." Harding was, apparently, too smart to risk a lie. "I was going to the men's room when I saw a bad egg heading for the library. I followed him because it was late in the afternoon on the last day of term. There'd been a search committee meeting, but there weren't too many people around. I was concerned about the women in the library."

"That was the responsible thing to do."

"Yeah. You wouldn't see Worth or Clawsen frog-marching some thug out of the Center."

"Which is what you did?"

"After a little palaver." Harding knelt to examine a piece of bark loosened at the base of a young tree. "Damn, I don't know what all is gnawing at my trees—rabbits, skunks, it's too low for deer. I didn't mention it because Donna asked me not to."

"Donna?"

"Donna Franchetti, one of the librarians. The tough guy is her ex-husband. Name's Tom Franchetti. Same last name as hers. F-r-a-n-c-h—"

"I can spell it," Nick said.

"Actually, I think there may still be some paperwork to do on the divorce. I was sort of sweet on her when she started working at the Center. Nothing serious"—Harding rose to his feet and walked on—"I'm a married man, but I like to shoot the breeze with a pretty girl . . . Anyway, I told this bozo to buzz off. He'd made a couple of scenes last fall, and the guards knew who he was. They had orders to keep him out."

"But he slipped past the guard at the front door?" Nick could ask Sam Sternberg how easily unauthorized visitors got into the Center.

"Yeah, or came in through the delivery entrance. He'd got in that way before. Delivers beer. He got in that way again yesterday."

"Yesterday? Was the Center open on New Year's Eve?"

"The Center doesn't close up completely, like the college. People can always get into their offices. The library was closing at noon and I went in to wish her a happy new year."

"Donna?"

"Sure, Donna. She's a nice girl. I like her. When I got there, I found this punk Franchetti shaking her and asking her what she was doing for New Year's Eve."

"Did she tell him?"

"No, she wouldn't. But she told me, after I threw Franchetti out, that she had a date with Richard Llewellyn. I stayed with her for a little while till she calmed down. She was worried about Dick and left a message for him at the BPL that Franchetti was looking for him."

"Did Franchetti know where Llewellyn was?"

"I don't know. Donna wouldn't have told him."

"Do you think he suspected she was seeing Llewellyn?"

"Llewellyn spent a lot of time with her."

"You observed that yourself?" Nick asked.

"Yeah, I did."

"And what did you think of Llewellyn?"

"Hell of a good kid. Real straight-shooter. Say, you know what he did?" They had moved on to a formal garden, the frosty air sharp with the smell of boxwood.

Denied you your rightful place in history, Nick thought. "No, tell me."

"He came right out with it—hell, I'd practically forgotten, happened so long ago. He wrote satire for his college paper under a pseudonym, and he did a real unflatterin' review of a book of mine that got circulated by some of my detractors. Boy told me it was too frivolous to list with his publications, but he wanted me to know."

"He must have trusted in your good nature."

"Maybe. Anyhow, it was damned fine of him to tell me." Harding stirred the gravel path with the toe of his riding boot. "We had a beer together and I told him in all sincerity I was grateful to him. I've made a ton more money consulting than I'd have made in Foggy Bottom."

Nick left Harding with a promise that he would do his best to recover the dagger, then stopped at a phone booth on the highway and spoke briefly to a judge he knew. When he finally got to the street where Tom Franchetti lived, he and two uniformed officers found Tom's bloodstained windbreaker in a garbage bag set out to be collected after the holiday. Across the street an empty trash can had been placed according to local custom to claim a parking place cleared of snow. At the bottom of the can lay a numbered key that looked like the kind that opened coin-operated lockers.

Hannibal tried the Boston Public Library itself, both railway stations, and finally, when it was nearly midnight on New Year's Day, the Greyhound Bus Terminal. In locker number 174 at the bus station, he found Harding's dagger stripped of all its emeralds and most of its opals. Two of the opals, softer than emeralds, had cracked and chipped.

ELEVEN

THE CASE FIT TOGETHER much too neatly, but the jacket and key were real and more than enough to justify holding Franchetti as a material witness, although there were constitutional issues about searching garbage for evidence. Some courts had held that the Fourth Amendment protected even discarded "papers and effects" from unreasonable search and seizure, so Nick, who hated to lose cases on technicalities, had taken pains with the language of the search warrant. He had a hunch incriminating objects would be found suggestively close to Tom Franchetti. The booking officer was amused that he'd been so careful. "Good thing you specified 'adjoining sidewalks and street.' The kid's a piece of garbage. He'll probably claim he lives in the trash, his can's his castle . . ."

Franchetti, surly and sniveling by turn, proved far less inventive. Nothing he said made sense.

"Franchetti's a miserable kid," Nick told Molly, after questioning him most of Monday, the second of January. "He's all bent out of shape."

"What did the psychiatrist say?"

"He said Franchetti was exhibiting paranoid posture."

"So it's unanimous," Molly said grimly.

"He recommended Franchetti be held without bail. He

thinks he's highly unstable and may bolt." Nick paced, thinking aloud. "Franchetti's not admitting it yet, but I'm fairly sure he went to the BPL to threaten Llewellyn and found him dead. That would account for the character of the bloodstains on his cuffs. You know the sort of absorbent ribbed cuff that glossy windbreakers have? The fabric hadn't been soaked by wet blood, just smudged by blood that had begun to dry."

"Maybe he took it off before he stabbed Llewellyn. It's the kind, isn't it, that has a team or club emblem and his name embroidered on the sleeve? That would provide such positive identification he'd be careful it didn't get stained."

"Could be."

"Yes, and after he put it back on, he might have tried to move the body someplace where it wouldn't be found until after the long weekend—and then heard someone coming and panicked." This case interested Molly deeply. Llewellyn belonged to a community she cherished, and she longed to avenge his death. "But you said Franchetti has an alibi for the early afternoon?"

"He was with his girlfriend."

"Alone?"

"Yes, and she's a pathetic, fearful little creature who'd say anything he told her to say," Nick said, "but the story rings true."

"What's his story?"

"Her parents, not surprisingly, do not like or trust him and they supervise her closely. If one of them can't keep an eye on her, her grandmother who lives around the corner is called in to chaperone. The only time their guard's relaxed is on Saturday afternoon when her father earns a little extra money tending bar and the two older women go, religiously so to speak, to bingo at Queen of Heaven."

"Also known as Our Lady of Perpetual Bingo."

"It's not one of Newnham's more enlightened parishes,"

he agreed. "There's no pressure to ordain women at Queen of Heaven. They aren't even allowed to call out the numbers at bingo parties."

"But women flock there all the same." Molly never ceased to be troubled by the slights, large and small, Catholic women bore.

"They do. And this girl's mother and grandmother never missed a Saturday." And so, as Franchetti had sullenly acknowledged, "the only time I get to bang her is when the old ladies are playin' bingo." Nick translated for Molly, "And so the lovers are alone only between two and four on Saturday afternoon, during the weekly bingo party at Queen of Heaven."

"Good lord," she exclaimed. "He couldn't have invented that detail. It's fantastic."

"My sheltered darling, of course he didn't make it up. It's a common predicament in Newnham, and he fell back on the traditional solution."

"Nick!"

"No," he answered her unspoken question. "I never resorted to it myself but I know people who did. Still, if Franchetti didn't linger over his lovemaking, he could have gotten to the library in time to kill Llewellyn. I don't think he's the murderer though."

The phone rang. "The coroner found a piece of opal in Llewellyn's lung," he said, after he hung up. "I asked him to look after I found the dagger." He could not bring himself to tell Molly the coroner had not found the chip at first because the dying man's convulsive coughing had forced it deep into his lung.

"Let's go for a walk. I can't sit still," she said. "I'm so angry. I can't believe either wretch, Franchetti *or* Harding, could have killed Llewellyn."

"Let's drive to the river and walk there."

They looked to the same things for solace and walked for

miles along the riverbank. Ice, milky and opaque, had formed close to the banks where the water was shallow, and ice extended in increasing transparency until it lay thin as crystal, framing the deep channel where the river ran swift and black. The rushing water struck the ice, making tinkling sounds, like glasses toasting the New Year. The gray sky was etched with bare boughs; the scene, one of uncompromising gloom. Only when they came close enough to a tree trunk to see lichen and moss could they believe color had not been drained from the earth. "It's still light," he said. "The days are a little longer than they have been."

"It's more than a week since the solstice," she understood he meant to comfort her. "I know no one is negligible and I'm sure Franchetti's griefs are very real. Still, this is a hard one."

"Any person, acting by stealth or with accomplices, can kill any other person. Some people, you know, regard that as the primary fact of social life."

"A bleak vision."

"And a true one," he said. "Do you think Harding prefers money to power?"

"I don't know. He's notoriously venal. He presents himself as growing up white trash lusting for hard cash. Actually, I've heard his father was a bank teller in some obscure county seat where his mother taught Sunday school. Genteel poverty doesn't make such a good story, but it's far more likely to make an academic."

"And a thin skin."

"Right. I think Harding would love glory," Molly speculated. "I think he plays the buffoon because it eludes him."

"I am virtually certain Franchetti didn't drop that key into an open trash barrel on his own street. He could so easily have dropped it in the river. Unlike the windbreaker, it would have sunk."

"Maybe he was in such a hurry to get rid of his jacket that he forgot about the key until he got home."

"He's unpolished and unstable, but he's not an imbecile. There's more going on here. A smart thief would have left the key in the locker. It certainly couldn't identify him. Let's cross at the next bridge and turn back."

On the footbridge, they met Margaret Donahue, and she introduced them to Jake Larson, with whom she had been gloomily staring into the dark water. Larson had learned of Llewellyn's death from Margaret when he'd returned from Kentucky that afternoon. Like Molly and Nick they preferred to mourn him out of doors. Nick confirmed the rumors they'd heard that Franchetti was in custody, and Larson, after the briefest pause, began, "Franchetti's hurting. I guess you ought to hear this story. You'll be a better judge of it than I am."

Larson told them that he'd arranged to go with Margaret to see her father's mural before he left town for the vacation. She'd invited him to supper and he'd been so busy getting ready for his trip he hadn't thought about buying a bottle of wine until he passed a liquor store a couple of blocks from the post office where he was meeting her. Franchetti accosted him while he was studying a shelf of indifferent California burgundies.

"Tom must have recognized me from the time he crashed the wine-and-cheese," Larson explained. "He assumed I was in Newnham to see Donna."

"You're sure of that?" Nick asked. "He confronted you?"

"He grabbed my arm. I ignored him and looked at a few more red wines."

"I'd told him steak was the only festive meal I knew how to cook," Margaret explained.

"I chose a zinfandel," Larson resumed, "and went to the front of the store to pay. Franchetti followed me. There was a girl with him, clinging to his jacket and begging him to leave me alone. He tried to grab the bottle out of my hand."

"What did he actually say?" Nick persisted.

"He said or I guess asked, 'You ballin' her too?' While he was trying to get hold of the wine, he said, 'You gotta get her shitfaced to do it?' And all the while this poor girl was pleading with him to stop."

"And he was so unconcerned about her," Molly proposed, "that he never even told her to shut up."

"Yes," Larson said, smiling. "Just like that. I shook him off once and he grabbed me again and promised to beat the crap out of me and all the other bastards at Marvell who were ballin' his wife."

"She's not his wife," Margaret interrupted angrily. "I don't know what it's going to take to convince him."

"I reminded him that Donna was getting a divorce, but he claimed that she didn't really want one. Marvell had given her funny ideas. He was going to set her straight. He finally threw a punch, but he's not much of a street-fighter."

"You're almost twice his size," Margaret said.

"I said he threw a punch," Jake explained. "Not that he landed one."

"You calmed him down?" Nick asked.

"I held him down, bent him over the counter by the cash register for a minute or two. He didn't seem out of control, and I asked the girl if she thought she could get him home. She said he was okay, she could take care of him, and I told her if she was sure he wouldn't give her any trouble, I wouldn't call the police. I thought he was her brother," he added. "She'd been so desperate to keep him out of trouble and he was so nuts about another woman. I asked her if their parents were at home, and she told me, in an embarrassed little voice, that she wasn't his sister."

Molly and Margaret looked at each other with pained resignation. These pathetic girls. For every young woman like Donna who fought her way to freedom, there were five in Newnham who'd rather be abused than ignored.

"God help her," Margaret said.

"It was awful," Larson agreed. "When she said she was his girlfriend, it really energized him. He hadn't struggled. He'd been completely cowed and I hadn't hurt him at all, just held him down. He spoke right up. 'Yeah,' he said, 'I ain't livin' like no fuckin' monk. I know Donna's gettin' laid. You think I'm a fuckin' moron?' "

"Cocky little shit." Margaret was almost beside herself.

"She didn't look more than fifteen. Younger than my daughter. I hated to leave her there."

"It's a sad story," Nick said. "But not damning. All the evidence against Franchetti is circumstantial."

"You didn't tell me about this," Margaret reproached Larson.

"I told Donna. I thought she was the one who had to be careful. I knew you were worried already. And vigilant."

"Not vigilant enough."

"Margaret, crime prevention's a good idea," Nick said. "But seldom possible."

They talked of their grief until the night grew very cold.

"Have you had dinner?" Molly asked finally. "We have the makings of a New Year's Eve supper we've been unable to eat. Why don't you come home with us?"

"Thanks," Margaret said. "You expect good food at a wake."

"Do you have any idea where the jewels might be?" Molly asked Nick the next morning. Conversation at supper had focused on Tom Franchetti and skirted the Center's possible connections with the tragedy.

"No," he said, "because I don't know who took them—the killer, whoever that may be, Harding, for reasons that may or may not be connected with the murder, or a thief innocent of Llewellyn's death who stripped the dagger and abandoned it.

The stones were removed before he was stabbed. We found traces of blood in the empty settings."

"Llewellyn's?"

"Yes, his type at any rate. What's Harding's marriage like? Do you know his wife?"

"Bitsy Harding"—Molly tried to phrase this honestly and without malice—"strikes me as intelligent but shallow and mercenary. I'm not sure what she feels for Bert, but she seems pleased she's been able to hang on to him."

"He arranged things so I wouldn't see her. He met me outside the house and kept me walking around his grounds and his carefully mulched gardens."

"Maybe he doesn't like her to meet attractive men."

"Maybe he doesn't like her to hear or talk about his weakness for attractive women. I'm going back to the public library this morning. You're finished packing, aren't you? Do you want to come?"

"Of course I'll come." Molly was leaving for Italy that night. Scattergood College gave generous sabbaticals and considerable flexibility in scheduling them. She'd originally planned to take off both terms, but early in the fall she'd found it impossible to leave. Murder had disrupted the congressional race in which she was keenly interested, and Nick's interest in her posed at that moment more troubling mysteries. The denouement had been entirely satisfying in both cases, but now the spring term and the postponed leave had begun and she must go. "I'm completely ready to leave tonight," she said. "Insofar as I could ever be prepared to leave you. I'd love to come with you."

The Boston Public Library imposed its elevating presence on Copley Square. Trinity Church looked like a Victorian sand castle, fantastic and ephemeral, faced with the library's granite fastness. Nor was there any doubt upon which faith the city relied: "The Commonwealth requires the education of the people as the safeguard of order and liberty" was the motto chiseled into its stone. A curious pantheon had been assembled, carved on its facade and steps, in support of this imperative: Epicurus, Heraclites, Augustine of Hippo, Rabelais, Francis of Assisi, Michelangelo, Correggio, Voltaire, Franklin, Darwin and scores of others.

Molly glanced at the names. "It must have been a lively meeting when they settled on that list."

"Some radical Republican probably nominated every writer on the Index," Nick said. "And the Democrats added a few literate saints and swarthy artists in a gesture of comity."

They entered the old building and climbed the Siena marble staircase bright as marigolds and surmounted by recumbent lions watching over the memory of Massachusetts volunteer regiments. The second-floor hall was long and dim, the main reading room cavernously dark on the first day after a holiday weekend: only a few diligent researchers had switched on reading lamps over a portion of library tables. They glanced in and then turned back down the hall to the foot of the steps that led to the top floor.

"Here," Nick said, "the stairway can be barred by this wooden lattice. It's an effective barrier because it's too high to jump and, unlike an iron grille, too light to support the weight of anyone attempting to climb over it. It can be padlocked, but it was open part of Saturday afternoon."

"The padlock could be picked, I suppose?"

"I imagine so, but it isn't scratched."

The upper hall was darker still, and there the lions of the Union yielded to a frieze of prophets and apostles glowing spectrally beneath a vaulted ceiling. "Painted by John Singer Sargent," Nick said. "It's called 'Judaism and Christianity.'"

"I've always liked it, but I don't think it suits the building."

"Suits the city," Nick countered, "it's a balanced ticket."

He took her hand and led her down the hall, past the chipped plaster, to the room where Llewellyn died. How easy it would be, she saw, to steal down that obscure hallway to the brass-studded leather doors of the Charlotte Cushman room, to watch your victim through the porthole windows until he was thoroughly engrossed in his work, and then, softly, pass through those discreet doors, made to minimize interruptions, and plunge a dagger into the back of a scholar intent upon his work. Molly felt again the grief and fury she first felt when she heard of Llewellyn's death. A stabbing in a foreign archive that had once been a palazzo would not be such a profanation, and there were historians, Molly could think of one or two, for whom it would not be a wholly unfitting end. But Llewellyn! Here!

"Where did you find the button?" she asked, after looking around the room carefully in an attempt to calm herself.

Nick showed her and speculated that it had hit the floor and bounced or rolled.

"The jacket hadn't been removed and then put back on, had it?"

"No, the dagger cut through it. I think the button was torn off when someone went through Llewellyn's pockets, including his inside pockets, hastily. His wallet and a small date and address book were in his inside breast pocket. There was money in the wallet, not a great deal but enough. I can't imagine, with the town full of tipsy tourists, anyone climbing to the third floor of the public library to roll a graduate student."

"Maybe someone was interested in the names and addresses."

"They'd have taken the book."

"Or photocopied whatever they wanted to know and put it back. There's a copying machine over there."

"Right"—he paused—"it does help to think aloud with you."

"Girls are brought up to be good listeners."

"You're much more traditionally feminine than you think,"

he said. "I'll miss you in lots of ways after you leave. Did I show you the notebook Llewellyn had with him?"

"Yes, but I wondered if that's all he brought with him. He must have had a parka or an overcoat. It was freezing on Saturday."

"We looked. He hadn't checked a briefcase or any outer clothing. The only things left in the cloakroom after the library closed were a shopping bag from F.A.O. Schwartz, full of children's books and jigsaw puzzles, and a few raincoats the attendant said had been there for months. And there aren't any lockers, except those belonging to the staff. I found that out when I was looking for the one the key from the trash barrel fit. They were all removed a few years ago during a spasm of concern for security after some bombs were left in airport lockers."

"He can't have been walking around without some kind of overcoat last Saturday."

"His claim check," Nick said. "That's what would have been in his pocket. The killer or someone who came later could have taken it and made off with whatever Llewellyn had left downstairs. And we'd never know because the plastic disc would be back where it's supposed to be, slipped over its hanger, indistinguishable from all the rest."

Nick and Molly went back downstairs and through the loggia to the new wing, where the philanthropists' names suggested a new era. They had an inconclusive talk with the cloakroom attendant who had worked the morning of New Year's Eve: he thought someone resembling Llewellyn checked a coat, but he himself had been off work at noon and the man who worked the afternoon was semi-retired and was driving to Arizona with his wife. That seemed a dead end.

They left the library through the Boylston Street entrance of the new building, passing the depository where borrowers could return books after the library closed. "Wait a minute," Nick said. "How often do you think they empty that box?"

"Lieutenant," the man in the cloakroom greeted them as they hurried back inside, "I told them you'd just left. They're looking for you down in the basement where the books are canceled."

A custodian checked the depository every morning. He was responsible for emptying and locking it at nine when the library opened, but he'd come in a little late. His morning routine was disrupted by gossip about the murder and it was nearly one o'clock before he'd gotten around to the depository. Few books were returned over the New Year's weekend, but someone had stuffed a wool-lined raincoat into the box. The coat rattled as he unfolded it. Unnerved by the murder, he dropped it on the floor and ran to get his supervisor who called the curator of prints, the library functionary who had dealt most recently with the police. The curator, still smarting from that encounter, was instructing everyone to remain six feet from the evidence until the police came, when Nick and Molly arrived. They heard the custodian's story, then Nick bent down and took from the coat pocket a boarding pass from United flight 335, Indianapolis to Boston, a sales slip from F.A.O. Schwartz, seven emeralds and four black opals.

"LIKE PEBBLES A CHILD GATHERED at the beach," Molly said, when they were alone in Nick's office. "Emeralds knocking around in his pocket. Margaret says she's certain it's Dick Llewellyn's coat. What did Bert say?" Molly had called Margaret and Nick had called Harding after they deposited the gems with a lab technician at police headquarters.

"He was grateful, fulsomely grateful and complimentary and in no hurry to get the stones back. Knows all about police procedure, understands they'll be kept as evidence, glad they're in good hands for the time being. He said his wife's determined to have them set in a necklace as soon as the trial's over."

"Franchetti's trial?"

"He's Harding's pick for murderer."

"People who check in library books must be creatures of habit," Molly mused, "and more than usually reliable."

"Yes, I can't think of a safer place to keep valuables over a long weekend than in a book bin. It would have been surprising if they hadn't been found and reported."

"What's this?" Molly saw a stack of heavy, new-looking books on Nick's desk. "Who would send you a book called *Proactive Approaches to Law Enforcement Administration?*"

"I ordered it and all the rest. Here, take a look at *Process-Oriented Structure in Police Management.*"

"What is this?"

"To pass the time while you're away I'm going to study for the captain's exam." He explained that eligibility for promotion to the rank of captain would depend upon the results of a two-hour multiple-choice examination based on these books. "Better than spoils, I suppose."

"I wonder," she said. "Of course, we know you test well."

"Other factors can be considered."

"What other factors?" she asked.

"There's a formula for factoring-in training and experience, and an Irish wife will be a definite plus."

"That's a motive I never suspected," Molly laughed. "I thought it only mattered in politics."

"Let's go home. We've only got a few more hours."

TWELVE

OLLY'S PLANE LEFT on schedule at nine o'clock, and Nick wanted to go anywhere but back home without her. Something had been troubling him all day. The coroner had described pretty graphically the sort of coughing fit that would have driven an opal chip into the tissue where he'd found it. How was it that the curator of prints hadn't heard it? The man had been very obliging. He seemed eager to atone for the folly, as he now understood it to be, of moving the body. He'd given the detective a home number that did not answer when Nick tried it from his office a little before ten. Nick left a message on his answering machine and settled down to the police management text-books.

About half an hour later, the curator returned his call. He had a ready and, to Nick, just then, an entirely credible answer. His wife had died about a year ago. He'd taken to eating his main meal at lunch with a glass of wine, perhaps two. He did not believe himself to be intemperate. Sometimes he dozed after lunch at his desk. He did not believe he abused his office. He invariably worked late, more than making up for the time spent napping. He preferred not to get home until he was tired enough to sleep. He had almost certainly slept longer than usual on the afternoon of New

Year's Eve, but the times he had given during their first interview were the correct ones to the best of his knowledge and belief. He'd talked with the young man shortly before two and discovered his body around four.

Nick told him he was sorry about his wife and glumly resumed studying. He'd made little progress when the phone rang again.

ALVIN WORTH RECOGNIZED his limitations. He knew he must enlist the help of others. He could no longer grapple with this unaided. Committed as he was to advancing the discipline of political science, he strove always to balance his responsibilities as a truth seeker and as a citizen. Moreover, he believed himself to be obliged under most circumstances to cooperate with the authorities. Therefore, with some trepidation, he had placed a telephone call to the Boston Police Department. He could hardly believe as an officer informed him his call was being recorded, that it was his own voice asking how he might contact a man he had met in Homicide. "Lieutenant Hannibal," he began, "this is Professor Alvin Worth. I did not expect to find you at your office at this hour, but I had something rather urgent to communicate. I had the pleasure of meeting you at a party given by Professor and Mrs. Sternberg."

"Yes, of course," Nick said. "You are seeking to introduce an ethical dimension into cost-benefit analysis." Phrases sometimes lodged themselves perversely in Nick's mind, and he had been unable to rid himself of several of Worth's.

"That's right," Worth replied, greatly pleased.

"You believe ethical values must be calibrated more precisely so that they can be seen to confer benefits as well as to impose costs." Nick repeated this almost against his will, because it had been dinning in his brain since he first heard it.

He knew political arguments were increasingly cast in cost-benefit terms, and he hoped there were efforts, other than Worth's, to give the new idiom some moral content.

Worth was astonished and flattered to have made so profound an impression on anyone. "I am most gratified," he said, "that you sympathize with my work. And I should be very grateful for a few minutes of your time."

"Shall I come to your office tomorrow?"

"I'd prefer that you came to my home."

"Certainly." Informants seeking that degree of privacy, Nick knew from experience, might be merely timid or self-important, but they were quite likely to be genuinely important.

"I don't suppose, it must be too much to ask, I've no idea what hours you work . . ."

"Would you like to see me tonight?"

"Very much."

ALVIN WORTH TOLD Hannibal, with many painful ellipses and disclaimers, that he had had during the winter vacation a houseguest, a young Thai graduate student, a very brilliant young man who was, as it happened, a candidate for the same job as the murdered man. He'd had some apprehensions about the boy's getting lost and so he'd taken to following him on his frequent walks around Boston. From time to time, these strolls had included the most uncongenial places. "I felt nothing but relief, I assure you," Worth said, "when he set out for the public library."

"And when was this?"

"On the afternoon of New Year's Eve. I lost him in the men's room, where I was not, frankly, comfortable loitering. He eluded me completely for almost forty minutes. I finally caught up with him in the crypt of Trinity Church." Worth knew he did right to unbosom himself of this burden. Norman Clawsen, in whom he would readily have confided, was still in Detroit, but he did not want to discuss this over the phone, and there was no one at Marvell other than Norman with whom he dared speak frankly about Tikibinitantari.

"Did you see or speak with anyone else at the library that afternoon?" Nick asked, after declining tea and sherry. Was Worth attempting to explain his own presence?

"No one." And certainly no one had, as yet, claimed to have seen him there.

"Would your houseguest have known where Llewellyn was working?"

"I cannot imagine how he would have known."

"But you knew yourself and might have mentioned it, perhaps in connection with some aspect of Llewellyn's research?"

"I myself did not know when Llewellyn would go to the BPL, only that it was his announced intention to do so at some point during the vacation. I'm not sure any of the other candidates knew even that."

"I'm grateful to you for telling me this," Nick said. "Very often small details that seem circumstantially damaging help us get the story straight. I wish you would tell me why, apart from the coincidence of his being in the library, you suspect this man."

"I am really torn." Worth was nothing if not conscientious.

"You're not a witness now," Nick continued. "You can speculate. I'd like to hear what you, as a man accustomed to moral reasoning, what you yourself sense."

Worth's Lhasa apso pattered into the room and nestled against his leg. Worth petted the dog nervously and then, in a gesture of almost despairing solicitude, gathered it up onto his lap.

"It fell to me. I am a bachelor. It fell to me to entertain the young man during the winter vacation. My colleague Norman Clawsen, whom I believe you also met at the Sternbergs' party . . ."

That was a wonderful memory, Molly's gaiety in refuting Marinetti. "Yes, he's very persuasive."

"Yes, a most committed scholar, and he would gladly have taken the boy, his name is Tikibinitantari, for part of the vacation." Worth and Clawsen both recognized that too much exposure would do the boy no good. "But Norman had to be in Detroit for the annual convention of the Association of Social Science Statisticians. I would have liked to go myself to hear about progress in the field, but it isn't strictly necessary for ethicists to attend." It was necessary, on the other hand, to monitor the young Thai who was immature, even for one so gifted.

Tiki, as he liked to be called, mostly read during the day or went for long walks. He seemed a hard worker, Worth told the detective: in a few hours he'd scanned every page the other candidates had submitted. "He took a lively, I would say even a combative, exception to their theories and expressed an eagerness to meet them."

Worth was becoming more and more uneasy and offered scotch. "I was alarmed the evening of his arrival by curious thuds that seemed to come from the guest room." He was holding his dog close to his chest now, with both arms locked around the animal.

"I knocked on his door and he readily admitted me. Lieutenant, he had drawn a large hermaphroditic figure on the wall in charcoal, and this target was studded with knives. He bowed, motioned me to a chair, removed the weapons and threw them again, unerringly, I might add."

The knife that struck Llewellyn had definitely not been thrown, but this was well worth hearing.

"I thought this merely eccentric until two sinister events coincided."

"I think I would like a drink," Nick said.

"I'll join you." Worth brought out a crystal decanter surmounted by a sterling silver stag's head and served a very good malt scotch.

"What were these two sinister events?"

"First, Fluff, my dog, disappeared, and then my garbage disposal jammed." Worth had searched his three-story townhouse for the little fellow and, since Tiki was out for a walk, looked also into the guest room, still adorned by the curious drawings. "Fluff is a curious little fellow, Lieutenant, and he often burrows into strange suitcases. I did not find him in Tiki's luggage, but I did find magazines with photographs that I do not judge to be protected by the First Amendment."

"And the garbage disposal?"

"You can imagine my horror. I struggled not to believe the worst, but when the repairman asked me whether any uncooked bones might have gotten into the works—he hadn't found anything yet but he said the obstruction, whatever it was, seemed not to be so brittle as roasted bones would be—I called California."

"California?"

"UCLA. Tiki's alma mater. I demanded to speak to the director of the university clinic. Some chit of a receptionist tried to tell me that the Family Educational Rights and Privacy Act forbade disclosure of any information from a student's medical record without the student's prior written consent, but I would not be diddled." Worth had actually said, "Cut the crap about FERPA." He was businesslike when his deepest feelings were stirred. "I demanded to know if effusive letters of recommendation written by their faculty had exposed me and mine to a homicidal maniac."

The receptionist had temporized and then put Worth

through to the chief of psychiatric services, who would volunteer no information but agreed to listen to a few questions.

"His answers were guarded," Worth told Hannibal. "He thought the boy's family provided him with a companion. He was usually accompanied by a man who looked like a wrestler. Finally, I put the real question. My heart was in my throat."

Nick leaned forward, all solicitude. "Was he responsive?"

"He said, I can hear him yet, 'I can positively assure you that his history indicates no interest in smaller mammals.' Beyond that, he held himself bound to silence."

Nick was speechless.

"I had no words to reply," Worth said. "And shortly thereafter, the repairman removed two silver coffee spoons from the disposal."

"And the dog looks perfectly all right." Molly would love the story about the garbage disposal. Worth looked like a man who measured out his life with coffee spoons.

"Fluff came home the next morning, rather dirty and shamefaced, but unharmed. But, I began to follow Tiki on his walks."

"You did the right thing," Nick said, "I appreciate hearing this. I know it's not easy for you."

"Lieutenant Hannibal," he faltered, "I could not swear to this. It was a most fleeting impression. But I also saw a man who resembled one of my colleagues in Copley Square that afternoon."

"Yes?"

"Not in the library itself, in the square."

"Not an unlikely coincidence."

"No, and not, you understand, in the library itself."

"I understand," Nick said.

"But, I rather thought, he appeared to be coming from the library."

"A natural place for a scholar to be coming from."

"A scholar, no," Worth said firmly, "Bertram Harding. Or perhaps someone who looked a great deal like him."

"Tall, portly?"

"Wearing a vicuña overcoat."

THIRTEEN

LVIN WORTH'S CONFIDENCES had taken up much of the night, and Nick's first morning without Molly was not given over to longing for her. He was awakened at six with the news that Tom Franchetti attacked the jailer who brought his breakfast and severely injured the man before other guards could subdue him. He had been transferred, heavily sedated, to Bridgewater, a state hospital for the criminally insane. Much of what he said during his preliminary evaluation convinced several doctors he would shortly confess to Llewellyn's murder. But the senior resident disagreed and diagnosed Franchetti's problem as shame, not guilt: he was mortified another guy beat him to it. Opinion among the orderlies and nurses split along similar lines.

At the Center for Participatory Politics, where classes resumed the next day, there was relief that the case was being held, for the moment, in abeyance, and much heated discussion of the insanity defense. Bertram Harding showed his concern for Donna in many ways and dictated to his wife a gracious letter inviting her and her children for a sleigh ride around their snowy grounds. Donna declined at first, so Bitsy Harding came to the Center herself to press the invitation. Their own children had gone back to their various schools, she said, and the big house seemed lonely without the stampede of young feet.

Donna believed Tom had killed Dick Llewellyn. She had warned Dick to beware of him. She knew Tommy watched her, but her own fears for herself had not extended beyond a beating. For Dick, maybe a brawl or a beating in which Tom's friends took part. She did not think he'd take Dick on alone, but she knew he could be cruel and violent and she was relieved he had been hospitalized. The distinction between madman and felon did not much interest her, nor did she reflect on the crime as it was reported in the papers. Life had taught her to concentrate on problems she could foresee and to set aside the griefs she had survived. Chiefly she worried about what she would say to her children as they grew older. It was not difficult to explain their father's absence: he visited them only to threaten her and rarely spoke to his daughters. But Donna dreaded the time when the girls would go to school and hear their classmates whispering that their father had killed their mother's boyfriend. In Newnham, nobody would say "lover."

Donna decided to accept the Hardings' invitation: her daughters might need influential friends if she wanted them to go to school outside Newnham or if Tom were ever released. She had long ceased to hope he would get better; now she feared he might get much worse. And the Hardings could not have been more cordial or reassuring. Bitsy Harding brought up the subject of country day schools the minute Andrea, the four-year-old, spelled out "cocoa" on the tin in the kitchen. They pressed Donna to stay the night and asked her to join them for a brandy after the children were in bed. She came downstairs and found them seated before an enormous hearth, drinking Armagnac out of gigantic brandy snifters. "You could roast an ox," Donna said.

"We do," Harding said laughing, "twice a year, Christmas and the Fourth of July. We hope you all come to the barbecue."

Talk became more serious as they drank, and more confidential. "Honey, you must be just sick with worry," Bitsy Harding said, "those bleedin' heart doctors will turn that maniac loose."

Donna admitted she dreaded Tom's release.

"I have friends on the state parole board," Bert assured her. "If we can get him sentenced, we can keep him locked up."

"Sentenced?" his wife asked sharply. "Wouldn't it be better to have him committed indefinitely?" It sounded as if she often gave Bert practical advice.

"Either way. Since nobody in this cloud cuckooland of a state's willing to think realistically about preventive detention, I'd like to see a conviction. But don't you worry, little lady"—Bert poured Donna more Armagnac—"you can count on us. We'll be looking out for you."

"It's the poor, honey," Bitsy said, echoing one of her husband's favorite points, "who suffer most from crime."

Donna nodded, uncertain whether they classed her with those unfortunates or, transformed by their patronage, among privileged persons unlikely to be victimized. "I wish it were over. You know what I mean, settled in some official way."

"Just between ourselves," Bert said. "I pulled a few strings out at Bridgewater and interviewed Tom myself. Then I had a word with the warden, told him to keep a sharp eye on Tommy."

"You think he's guilty?" Donna asked. "You're sure?"

"My mind has come to rest."

NICK HANNIBAL'S MIND had not come to rest, and he too paid a visit to Bridgewater State. Tom Franchetti, with almost no prompting, tearfully confessed that he had failed to kill Dick Llewellyn. Maybe the drugs they were giving him made him maudlin. He'd meant to kill Llewellyn, set out for the public library intent on murder, but he'd missed his chance. "All them rooms. It took me an hour to find him," Franchetti sobbed. "Friggin' mausoleum. Looked like it shoulda been full of corpses."

Someone who knew the BPL better, Hannibal reflected, would have found Llewellyn easily, particularly if he knew which collection he was working on. "Tom, I want to hear everything you've got to say, but I think you'd better have a lawyer with you. Do you have a lawyer now?" Some days before, Franchetti had dismissed his first court-appointed lawyer, an elegant young woman fresh from Yale Law School.

"Yeah, another dame. If this one screws up, can I get a guy?" A veteran public defender, henna-haired and chain-smoking, had replaced the pretty Yalie. After three minutes with Franchetti, she told him he'd never see a woman in a bedroom or in a kitchen again—he'd probably never see the outside world again—unless he told her the whole truth fast. She'd taken his case on a dare from her staff and she'd much prefer to spend the time with Asian immigrants who thanked you for your trouble. Tommy had grudgingly accepted her help and now handed Nick the card she had left with him. When Nick called her, she agreed to meet him at the hospital the next afternoon.

"You were seen at the Center at Marvell just before noon," Nick began his formal questioning. The lawyer listened impassively, watching her client's reactions as he sat on the edge of his iron bedstead. They were meeting in Franchetti's cell-like room, an isolation chamber more secure than a consulting room.

"Donna tell you that?"

"No. Were you there?"

"Yeah."

"And where did you go next?"

"To the bus station."

"You said yesterday you went straight from the Center to the public library."

"The station's on the way," he shrugged. "Besides I hadda know I could get away afterward, didn't I? I checked the buses to Fall River."

She must be sure he's not guilty, Nick thought, to let him admit that degree of premeditation. "That makes sense. Did you have a weapon?" The theft of the dagger had been kept quiet; Harding feared its loss wouldn't sit well with the emir.

"I didn't need no weapon. I coulda killed him with my bare hands."

Nick judged that an unlikely outcome of a fight between the two men. Llewellyn's body had looked strong and well exercised, and several people, Margaret Donahue and her friend Larson among them, had mentioned Franchetti was easily faced down. "No weapon?" he repeated.

Franchetti looked inquiringly at his lawyer, who nodded brusquely. Folding chairs had been provided for her and for the detective. She had settled immediately into one of them, either long used to its discomfort or indifferent to it. Nick remained standing, pacing as he questioned the suspect, pausing to hear his answers. "I had a tire iron in my truck," Franchetti said. "I wasn't gonna use it on him. I took it in case I had trouble gettin' away. I didn't know, like, how many bouncers there'd be. Where Donna works, they have a lot of 'em."

"So you took a tire iron into the library with you?"

"Yeah. I had it under my jacket."

"And you smashed the corridor wall with it after you saw Llewellyn's body?"

"I felt lousy."

Probably felt faint, Nick thought; he couldn't have much experience with dead bodies.

"He's not a murderer." His lawyer drew the same conclusion. "What he saw shocked him."

"Did you see anyone you recognized at the bus station?" Franchetti shook his head. "In or around the public library?"

He thought maybe a couple of guys. The medication he was taking clearly interfered with his concentration, but he eventually produced an unmistakable description of Bertram Harding and an equally full picture of another man: short, broad-shouldered, red-faced, with a graying, thinning crew-cut.

"Pink-cheeked with the cold?" Nick asked. No, Franchetti recognized the color as a more lasting alcholic rose, and he was pretty certain he worked at the Center, too. Franchetti grew drowsier, remembered nothing more, and dozed off.

"I wouldn't attach much importance to his sightings of Marvell professors," the lawyer cautioned, as she waited with Nick for an orderly to see them out. "He's a little fuzzy, as you saw, and even when he's completely lucid, academics must look pretty much alike to him."

Hannibal didn't know what to make of her advice. Franchetti wouldn't be off the hook until a more convincing suspect turned up. On the other hand, he'd already met Bert at close enough range to describe him and to dislike him thoroughly; the suspicion he was trying to pin the crime on someone else would not help to clear him.

On balance, Nick judged the leads worth pursuing. He went to the Center for Participatory Politics and found Margaret and Jake Larson in the cafeteria working on an exercise from Norman Clawsen's *Crisis Situation Simulation* workbook. They were both ready for a break. Jake got another pot of coffee, and as they drank it Nick asked them who around Marvell was small, strong-looking and perpetually flushed.

They agreed it sounded like Emory Stokes. "His office," Margaret said, "is upstairs, next to the dean's."

Emory Stokes's office reminded Hannibal of those restaurants blanketed with celebrity photographs to distract their patrons from the indifferent prime rib. A picture behind Stokes's desk succeeded in distracting him for a full minute until he concluded that the third man sitting with James Michael Curley, Gloria Swanson and Henry Cabot Lodge likely *was* the young Richard Nixon.

"I have friends everywhere," Stokes said, pleased by the interest Nick took. "This crowd at Marvell, they'd trade any of their degrees for my contacts." Stokes had earned a bachelor's degree at a state teachers college near Topeka, from whence he'd organized four Kansas counties for Thomas E. Dewey in 1948. He'd gone to Washington after graduation, left public service in 1961, then briefly returned to it in the early seventies. He told people he was working on two books, his reminiscences and a more theoretical work, *Strategies of Damage Control.* From time to time he spoke of combining the two projects.

"I like to see a fellow with practical ability," he said in reply to Nick's question. "Certainly I followed Bert when he left here on New Year's Eve. I'm a man of the world myself, but Bert is reckless. I'm careful about appearances for Bert's own good and for the good of the Center. We can't have our biggest asset brawling with a jealous husband, a jealous honest-to-God blue-collar, dues-paying Teamster husband. It's just too much." He struck his forehead with the heel of his hand. "Too much! And over a woman less than half Bert's age with two small children." Stokes appeared well up on the Franchetti family.

"You assumed his quarrel was with Tom Franchetti?"

"Of course. Actually, he said he was going into Boston to see you about the theft of his dagger."

"He *said* he was going to see me, not the police in general?"

"Yes, I remember because I made some joke about elephants. But I didn't believe him. I thought he was going after Franchetti, so I asked him for a lift into town."

"And you made up an errand?"

"I had a legitimate errand—nipping into Brooks Brothers to pick up my new blazer. Slubbed silk, the color of ripe raspberries." Stokes took pleasure in sartorial detail. "They were substituting monogrammed buttons, and it was supposed to be ready at noon on New Year's Eve. Bert parked on Newbury Street. I went in the side entrance of Brooks Brothers and out the front door in time to see him turn toward Copley Square instead of continuing along Berkeley Street to police headquarters."

"And you persevered?" Nick gave Stokes high marks for diligence.

"Why do anything halfway? Unfortunately, I'm not as fast on my feet as Bert. By the time I got to Copley Square, he was leaving the BPL."

"You're sure he'd actually been there?"

"I inferred that," Stokes said testily. "I saw him descending the front steps."

"About what time?"

"Three o'clock. He walked down the library steps and headed for the Copley Plaza, where he took the elevator to the sixth floor. I thought I could safely leave him there." Stokes obviously wanted to explain how he'd reached that conclusion.

"As a man of the world?" Nick was happy to indulge him.

"Let me tell you," Stokes's face flushed redder with pleasure. "I was mighty resourceful. I went to the hotel flower shop and ordered two dozen roses for a lady I thought might be staying there. I figured if Bert wasn't going down to Washington, she'd come up. When I gave her name, the manager said, 'Certainly, sir, she's in suite 610. We'll run them right up.'"

"Your extravagance disarmed them," Nick said. "Homicide couldn't afford it, though, as a regular ploy."

"No point, I always say, in doing anything halfway. I signed the card 'an admirer.' But, listen, Lieutenant"—Stokes turned suddenly surprisingly grave—"there's no reason to involve the lady. Her husband's one of the worst tomcats on the Hill and Bert does her a world of good."

"You were convinced, anyway, he'd be busy for the rest of the afternoon."

"Absolutely certain," Stokes said with finality.

"Do you remember what Harding was wearing?"

"Glen plaid suit, ecru silk shirt made by the London haberdasher who makes all his shirts, Grenadier Guards tie—gift of Mrs. Thatcher—his Monroe Doctrine overcoat, of course, and a new scarf he got for Christmas, cashmere on one side, madder silk on the other."

"Shoes?" Nick asked. Stokes himself wore well-polished oxblood wingtips that looked handsewn. A pair of galoshes stood beneath his trenchcoat on a coat rack near the office door.

"I don't remember," Stokes admitted, seemingly chagrinned by this lapse. "Most likely loafers, Swiss or Italian."

"Doesn't anybody around here wear boots in the winter?"

"Sam Sternberg does, because he sometimes walks to work. So does Alvin Worth. So do I. All of us with lifestyles less grand than Bert order heavy-soled snowboots from the same woodsy catalogue. But it was New Year's Eve," Stokes reminded the detective. "He didn't plan on being outdoors much. Now that I think of it, I'm pretty sure he had on Gucci loafers. Bert has plenty of lord-of-the-manor rural footwear, but he never wears it in town."

"The boots you all order. Do you have a pair here?"

"Why, yes, as a matter of fact," Stokes said with an ingratiating smile. "A new pair just arrived." Stokes opened a box on his desk and handed Nick an L.L. Bean boot, obviously never worn, its sturdy sole scored with a pattern of snow-gripping Vs. "There must be dozens of these around," he said.

"Hundreds," Nick said. "Thanks for your help. One last thing—" He paused at Stokes' office door. "Harding's dagger's something of an oddity here, isn't it? People don't generally keep lethal weapons in their offices?"

"Could somebody reasonably expect to find a weapon here?" Stokes looked sharply at the detective. "Somebody other than its owner? Is that what you're getting at?"

"Yes."

"Not these days." Stokes seemed to speak with genuine regret. "A lot of World War II veterans hung on to their sidearms. An old guy who taught political theory collected Confederate cavalry sabers, took 'em to class when he lectured on Calhoun. But not anymore. They're not a very colorful bunch, Lieutenant, the guys who do politics at Marvell. Bert's the only gun fancier left."

Candid as Harding had been, Nick thought, he'd omitted to mention that.

"It's funny," Stokes continued. "Harding keeps a valuable collection of antique weapons in his office. He's never kept them at home because his wife is afraid their kids will get at them."

"Is this generally known?"

"It's no secret, and he keeps them in a locked case, naturally. Handguns, curiosities mainly, a stiletto pistol, a revolver that shoots darts, things like that."

"But they're locked away, out of sight?" Nick asked.

"That's right. Whoever took the dagger may not have known they were there. Or he may have known most of them weren't in working order, or . . ." Stokes paused portentously.

"Yes, or what?"

"He, or she, may have chosen the most conspicuous one, the one that was the most embarrassing for Bert to lose."

Stokes looked at his watch. "You'll excuse me, Lieutenant, I have to meet a lady at six."

"Certainly. I'm grateful for your time"—Nick handed him a card—"and your insights. You can reach me anytime at this number."

"Thank you." Stokes tucked the card into his billfold. "I'll call you if anything else occurs to me."

"I'd appreciate that."

Nick went back to his office after questioning Stokes and reviewed his notes on the case. It was dark before he finished, a starry, windy night when he would have liked to walk along the river with Molly. It was midnight in Florence now, but she'd be awake.

"I was thinking of calling you," she said. "But I wasn't sure where you'd be. Listen to something I found in the archives today." And she read him a letter written by a prisoner of the Inquisition to his wife: lyrical tenderness alternated with staunch and ingenious heresy. He praised her mouth and her breasts, advanced several arguments against the existence of angels and exhorted their children, daughters as well as sons, to work hard on their Greek.

"Sounds as if your day was pleasanter than mine. I found out for certain that not only Worth and Tikibinitantari, but also Harding and somebody called Emory Stokes were around the public library on December thirty-first. It must have been like a French farce: in and out of bathroom stalls, behind pillars, in one door and out the window."

"And you think it's one of them."

"I've never thought Franchetti was bloodstained enough or in the right places. And he didn't get rid of the clothes he was wearing underneath the windbreaker on Saturday because he still had them on when we picked him up. There may be some explanation for that. I'm not sure."

"Is there anything else new?"

"Nothing is ever new in Homicide, nothing under the sun.

A few professional killings, some misunderstandings between friends, aggravated by drink or dope, one predictable but elusive psychotic and all the spontaneous domestic violence that comes with the waxing and waning of the holiday spirit."

"My spirits are waning a bit," she said wistfully. "It was heavenly living with you."

"You set a high standard for domesticity, babe. I can't wait for it to start again."

FOURTEEN

UDREY CLAWSEN DREADED her husband's return from conventions. She believed that Norman met other women when he traveled. She was sure of it because, unfailingly, he returned with variations on the conjugal act—innovations so awkward and uncomfortable that she longed for the day, never too distant, when he'd begin to neglect her again. But this time it seemed she would be spared erotic novelty. Norman had been too preoccupied to fool around. A review of his new book appeared in a journal on the very eve of the convention and it must have upset him a great deal. Audrey no longer attempted to read his books or reviews of them, but she had overheard Norman talking on the phone with Alvin Worth the night he came home.

For a few minutes they discussed the murder of the young man neither of them had liked. It was a sad thing, she heard Norman say, truly regrettable. The fellow lacked the rigor Marvell demanded, but he was not without ability. He might have had a thoroughly respectable career at some lesser institution and, in time, done useful work. His voice dropped then, and Audrey thought they were talking about Bertram Harding.

When the conversation became audible again, she heard her husband say he had given up trying to reply to the wretched review. He had written several drafts and finally decided it would be more dignified to ignore the bitch and hope for more intelligent reviews in more important journals from scholars better qualified to comment on his work. Then Norman listened for a long time to whatever his friend was saying. "That's a good idea," he said finally. "Gresham's adviser would be the perfect man. He's on the editorial board of *Binary Politics* and he owes me one."

When Norman was asleep, she let herself into his study and found, on his desk, a clipping she thought must be the one that had upset him. "It would be hard to find," she read,

a more mechanical application of unsuitable techniques to sensitive matters. Indeed, it would be impossible even to imagine manipulations less likely to prompt any individual or body to yield up its secrets. Clawsen has shown once again a perverse genius for probing areas peculiarly unresponsive to his clumsy assaults.

Audrey could scarcely believe her eyes. That was exactly what it was like, and a woman had written it. Norman must have slept with her. Some smart, shameless woman had gone to bed with Norman and told the world how it felt. Served him right. Served her right too, going to conventions with other women's husbands. She had probably led him on.

Tears blurred her vision for a few minutes. When she resumed reading, she gasped at the next sentence. "Clawsen's risible efforts . . ." ! Did *risible* mean partially impotent? She consulted the dictionary on Norman's desk and was relieved to find the word meant, simply, laughable. Laughable, she thought was not the first word she would have chosen to describe her husband.

Before she left the room, she checked his calendar. "Margaret Donahue" was penciled in for lunch on the following

Wednesday. Another woman! She was mildly surprised that Norman had not given up on women.

MARGARET DONAHUE HUMMED TUNELESSLY as she painted. She had two hours of the morning left before she had to clean herself up and meet Norman Clawsen for lunch. She assumed he intended to lobby her on behalf of George Gresham, and she would have preferred to continue with her work. In her opinion, the search, suspended after Llewellyn's death, ought not to be resumed until the fall. Certainly neither Gresham nor that odd young Thai had anything interesting to say for himself. Margaret squeezed some paint onto her palette and stabbed her brush purposefully into the shining coil.

She had decided during the winter vacation to take a studio art course next term. After all, she had come to Marvell to broaden herself, and she had not found time for years, for decades, she now realized, to paint or draw. She had continued to teach after she became chairman of the art department; even when she also took on the presidency of the teachers' local, she put in time in the classroom. That was a matter of principle with her. But it had been ages since she had been alone with a brush or pencil in her hand.

Margaret's paintings were bold and violent. She felt an affinity for the Expressionists and used harsh colors much like theirs. People forced as she was always to compromise and placate, to settle for half a loaf and the lesser evil, were constantly, she reflected, stifling the impulse to scream.

Jake Larson had smiled when she confided this. "I don't know who'd strike you as tough, if you think you're soft. I bet you drive hard bargains."

Margaret recognized that her art was escapist. It was, in that sense, unlike Jake's. His drawing grew out of his work and, he claimed, helped him with it. During meetings, while people thought he was doodling, he drew caricatures. The sketches he made struck her as savagely perceptive.

"Drawing a person helps me figure him out," he had admitted slyly when he showed them to her. "I started doing it the first time I had to deal with Chrysler."

"I know Worth feels contempt for us," she said. "But I've never seen him express it openly."

"Not in our meetings. This was during Dick Llewellyn's talk."

"Interesting." She had gone through the sketches carefully, nodding in vigorous recognition as she paged through his notebook. "That's the knowing look Stokes puts on when he's completely baffled. And you've got Harding right, too. There's an uneasiness beneath his bluster."

"All of them, except Sam, look anxious most of the time. Have you noticed that?"

"Yes, and I can't imagine what they're afraid of."

"Maybe they're afraid they'll be lopped off the cutting edge."

Margaret, and this was characteristic of her, never asked if Jake had drawn her. It never occurred to her, although they spent part of almost every day together; Margaret felt her life falling again into the full but unhurried rhythms of her own high school days. High school, not college. College had been frantic: studying on the trolley, practice-teaching, waiting on tables nights and weekends, helping her worn and resentful mother nurse her father through his last agonizing illness. High school, in contrast, had been patterned and carefree. There had been lots to do but time to do it all. She had thought in those days she could do everything. Pursue art and justice simultaneously. Fall in love.

And though there was little physical resemblance, eating in the Center's cafeteria reminded her of high school lunch period. The Newnham High School gym had doubled as a lunchroom; basketball hoops with tattered netting hung from smudged cement-block walls that were ineffectually freshened in August of alternate years with a dull green wash. Cement block she remembered as the building material most employed in the underfunded schools of postwar Newnham. In those years anyone who could afford it moved to the suburbs, and Newnham became a city of the working poor. Plants, not basketball hoops, hung from the subtle taupe walls of the Center's cafeteria, plants and tasteful graphics. The food was excellent, generously subsidized by conscious policy—the notion being to foster camaraderie by encouraging everyone to eat there.

But however exquisite the salad bar, however imaginative the soups, they produced little fraternization. As in Newnham High School, the long lunch tables were occupied solely by one sex or the other. The older secretaries ate by themselves. Better dressed, though seldom better educated younger women—administrative assistants and research aides—sometimes lunched with junior faculty, but, in general, they did not. Full professors rarely ate there at all: they went to the Faculty Club unless pressed for time between a noon lecture and a two o'clock seminar. Occasionally they asked students or midcareer fellows to lunch with them at the club; and that, Margaret gathered, was a much-prized condescension. She had been amused by the portentousness with which Norman Clawsen extended his invitation to her. Twelve-thirty, she noted with exasperation; how quickly the morning had gone.

Nearly always, she had lunch with Jake, sometimes Lou Stillman joined them, and one day Margaret realized that, in contrast with her high school status as a tall, plain, smart, undesirable girl, she had become, here at Marvell, one of the few women who daily lunched with a male friend. Thirty years ago, only the prettiest and most self-confident girls detached themselves from the feminine gaggle and ate in public with their boyfriends. There was, of course, nothing romantic about her friendship with Jake.

He had told her a few days after they first met that he was divorced. That wasn't a scandal, these days, just a census category. Single. Married. Divorced. Widow/er. She had told him on the same occasion that she had never married. Single. A different box on the form. Neither of them had inquired, subsequently, beyond that. The Center's optional personal information questionnaire circulated by Emory Stokes had been more intrusive; it offered three additional possibilities: Separated or Contemplating Separation, In Relationship, and Other.

But Margaret herself had grown curious. Why would a man who seemed so thoroughly reliable leave his wife? It was some days after she began to reflect on this question that she turned it the other way round and when she did she found it impossible to imagine that his wife had left him. Margaret knew odd things happened in marriage, but what fault could a woman have found with Jake?

She revolved this question in her mind as she methodically cleaned her brushes. It continued to puzzle her as Jake sat quietly down on the stool beside the sink. "I came to take you to lunch. I forgot you were eating with Norman Clawsen today."

"I wish I could forget it too. What have you been doing this morning?"

"Reading about Samuel Gompers," he said. They were both continuing with the second semester of a labor history course taught jointly by a historian and a sociologist. Jake was writing a paper about Gompers, the first president of the American Federation of Labor, who, asked what workers wanted, stated their agenda simply: "More."

"I'm doing Emma Goldman," she said.

"You would. She's more inspiring. I'll walk you to the Faculty Club."

It was a good distance from the fine arts building to the Faculty Club, and they walked briskly to get there by one. "Irene always reminded me of Samuel Gompers," Jake said as they neared that monstrous brick pile.

"Who's Irene?"

"My ex-wife. I've never seen a more honest and unapologetic materialism."

"I'll be at the Center this afternoon." She was eager to hear him out but afraid to be discourteously late for lunch. "I expect I'll run into you."

"Ms. Donahue," Norman Clawsen greeted her in the foyer. He took her coat ceremoniously, searched at length for a hanger on the crowded racks outside the dining room, demanded a table by a window and recommended the oyster stew. "Of course, you're a New Englander by birth. You probably know this menu better than I do," he tittered. "What would you recommend?"

"Scrod."

"Excellent. Broiled, for two," he gave their order. "And wine?"

"You choose."

He ordered an expensive white burgundy. After sampling it and nodding his approval, he told her that George Gresham's work was very important and that, in his wide experience, it was remarkable for lay persons to ask questions as discerning as her own about such highly technical material. "You have a real gift," he said. "George had hoped to join us, but he's been unavoidably detained. He asked me to tell you he's benefited immensely from your criticism."

"That's nice of him. I didn't think I'd been very helpful." Margaret had not seen the point of Gresham's research and had said so several times.

"You forced him to think it through afresh. 'Afresh,' that was his word."

She believed it wasn't Clawsen's. Worth's most likely.

"Tragic though," he continued, "that the search brought a young man here to his death."

"It is an appalling tragedy. Dick was so eager and vital."

"Yes," Clawsen's assent lacked warmth. "Eager. I suppose he told you about the project he was eager to do next?"

"Transitions from farmer to labor activism, I think. The politics of newly urbanized workers."

"He wouldn't have broken any new ground with that, I'm afraid. Harding looked into those issues a bit, for the Chileans. He helped the junta anticipate problems and nip them in the bud."

"I don't think that's what Dick had in mind."

"No doubt you're right." He laid his napkin on the table and leaned forward confidentially. "Would you like to have coffee upstairs in the library? It's a very private sanctum."

"I'd love a cup of coffee."

"Beautiful wood, isn't it?" Clawsen said, as they went up the winding staircase.

"Yes," she paused to admire the golden oak. "But it doesn't have those little brass fittings."

"What fittings?"

"Haven't you seen them?" she asked. "They're quite a fixture of nineteenth-century Boston. Small triangular pieces of brass set into each step where it meets the wall—in case the Irish maids couldn't be trusted to get into the corners."

"Or to spare the dear girls the trouble. Where can they be found today?"

"The dear girls?"

"No, the brass pieces."

"I first saw them at the Somerset Club." She hadn't said it to put him down, to "send a signal," as he would say, that she'd been taken to better clubs. A certain ambience unfailingly reminded her of those dust guards; they irked and amused her and she mentioned them whenever they came to mind. Clawsen bit his lips in vexation, and she tried to make amends. "I've been there only once. A very decent Brahmin, the last one to serve on the school committee, was retiring and there was a party. "

"I've never been there," he said bitterly.

"How was lunch?" Jake asked. They were studying in his rooms, as they often did. Midcareer fellows who chose to live at the Center had small suites, a largish sitting room with a desk and commodious bookshelves and an adjoining bedroom and bath.

"Okay, if you like frozen scrod. Clawsen took me up to the library afterward to warn me, in strictest confidence, that Bert Harding's intentions were never honorable."

"Toward you?"

"No, toward Donna Franchetti. He suggested that a woman who knew something of the world ought to warn her. He was reluctant to undertake so delicate a mission himself, he said."

"That's interesting. Worth took me aside half an hour ago to say that Harding favored abolishing the minimum wage."

"Samuel Gompers wouldn't like that." Margaret blurted this out. She had found it hard to listen to Clawsen, impatient as she was to hear about Jake's divorce.

"My daughter Karin's getting married on the Saturday after Valentine's Day. I guess it's been on my mind a lot." He spoke apologetically. "Karin as a little girl, and my wife. Do you mind if I tell you about it?"

"I wish you would."

"I was a disappointment to her." Jake was conscious of her full attention and grateful for it. "I lost my job. I was teaching high school physics and we went to Sweden for the summer with a bunch of kids on an exchange program. I thought we'd never been happier. When we got back the local Rotary Club invited me to show my slides. One of the doctors in the club asked how socialized medicine worked and I said I thought it worked fine. The word got round pretty fast that I was a Red."

"Yes, I can't see this nostalgia for the fifties," Margaret said.

"Irene, my wife, was very upset. Her brother ran a weekly paper, and they both wanted me to recant, or at least to write an article attacking some other aspect of Swedish society."

"Naturally you refused."

"Yes, and just as naturally, in the spring, my contract wasn't renewed. Irene expected I'd earn a doctorate in education, get to be principal and eventually superintendent of schools."

"That wouldn't have been difficult."

"You mean those jobs always went to any man in the system who wasn't a total turkey?"

"That was the pattern," Margaret said. "Still is."

"It was Irene's plan anyway—Doctor and Mrs. Larson. When I lost my teaching job, I went to work in a factory. It paid well and I got involved with the union. The union took up a lot of my time." He ran his hand through his grizzled hair; the low afternoon sun shone through the golden hairs on the back of his hand and the darker reddish hair of his head. He wore a red plaid shirt and, she thought, radiated warmth.

"Your wife probably missed having you at home. You must have been working much longer hours."

"She didn't want my company. She wanted me to study engineering at night, but I liked what I was doing. The union mattered to me. I was making more money than I'd ever made before. We were living better than ninety percent of the people in the world."

"But not better than ninety percent of the people she knew."

"That's right. What do they call it here, when you're still dissatisfied even though you're not really needy?"

"Relative deprivation."

"Irene was a real pioneer in experiencing that. When our daughter was ten, she needed braces on her teeth. We could afford them. We weren't poor. One weekend I went to a meeting in Chicago and Irene flew to Barbados with Karin's orthodontist. His wife had left him for a cardiologist."

"Land of opportunity." Margaret shook her head in sympathy and disapproval.

"I was very angry. I knew she wasn't happy about the things I was doing, but I never thought she'd sell herself so she could live in nine rooms instead of six."

Margaret nodded.

"Then I had a really lousy affair with a woman at the plant. But the marriage was past saving before that. Irene bettered herself. That's actually the way she talked about it."

Margaret talked about her private life with no one, but now the symmetry of their friendship seemed to call for an answering confidence. "I was engaged briefly to a man your wife would approve of. He was very up-and-coming."

"But you broke it off?"

"It was mutual—a simultaneous and easily foreseen bust-up."

"Chemistry wasn't right?"

"Maybe. I never learned the lingo for describing failed relationships. I only had the one. We fought about Joe McCarthy and the Episcopalians."

Larson laughed. "You're wonderful, Margaret. I never even heard about McCarthy attacking them."

"I don't know that he did. Our quarrel was more personal. This guy was an Irish Catholic Young Republican, and ideology and ambition were tugging him in different directions. He believed Catholics were stauncher anti-Communists but he was equally certain you met a better class of people as an Anglican."

"A dilemma," Larson chuckled. "How'd he resolve it?"

"He didn't resolve it," she said scornfully. "He wanted a showy Catholic wedding in Newnham to please his mother and to keep his options open if he ever decided to run for office there. Then, once we were married, he thought we should move out to the suburbs and join an Episcopal church. I wasn't wild about either prospect, but I was positively revolted by the idea of combining them."

"Did you love him?"

"I guess so. But I couldn't imagine living the sort of life he wanted. My mother was furious with me, and my sister thought I was crazy to let him get away. She married him herself a couple years later."

"So you did other things."

"I like what I do."

"So do I," he said.

There was a knock on the door, and he stooped to kiss the top of her head before he answered it.

"Glad to find you both here. Hope I'm not intruding," Bert Harding said, making himself at home on the couch next to Margaret. "We're having a little get-together, a house party, so that we can really get to know each other, out at our place next weekend. I hope you all will come out."

"I'm going home," Larson said. "My daughter's getting married."

"Jeez, how's it feel to be the father of the bride?" He did not wait for an answer. "How about you, Maggie?"

"I'm free. I'm almost certain I can come. Thank you."

"Great. I hoped you'd say that." He handed her a photocopied map with admirably clear directions to his house. "See"—Harding smiled, as he got up to leave—"I came prepared. See ya. Say—" He turned at the door and stepped back into the room. "What's the word in your town, Maggie?

Do people think Franchetti's guilty? I'm hearing the police aren't so sure."

"Some folks are sure he did it, others are sure he's innocent."

"They'll have a hell of a time finding unbiased jurors, won't they? See ya soon," he waved and left.

"What's he up to?" Margaret asked.

"You'll have to find out and tell me. Will Franchetti be hospitalized until the trial?"

"He's in for a forty-day observation period. Nick Hannibal —you remember, the detective we had dinner with—thinks that whatever the doctors recommend, bail will be set very high. He won't be able to raise it and nobody else will raise it for him."

"Do you think he killed Dick?"

"He tried to kill another boy when he was fifteen."

"With a knife?"

"Yes. I didn't see the fight, but the gym teacher who broke it up told me about it. He was an ex-marine and no alarmist. After what I heard from him, I insisted Tommy be expelled."

"And you've befriended Donna and told her to persevere without him," Larson said. "I'm beginning to be as glad as Harding seems to be that he's out of circulation."

FIFTEEN

BITSY HARDING, MORE LAVISHLY MADE than most women who choose to wear white, greeted her guests in a tight-bodiced, full-skirted wool crepe dress embellished with flounces and the hint of a bustle: part Regency barmaid, part *grande dame,* all hospitality. She carries it off, though, Margaret Donahue thought, you have to give her that. Mrs. Harding stood, like a regal pigeon, bosom forward, weight resting on the balls of her tiny feet, shod in white suede and set firmly on the black and white marble tiles of the Hardings' entry hall. Four strands of white pearls and two of black coiled on that rich bosom and baroque pearls hung weightily from her ears.

"Miss Donahue," she cooed. "May I call you Margaret? My husband's a great admirer of yours, but I'll let him speak for himself. Lord knows, he's not bashful. Here, sugar"—she handed Margaret's bag to Bert. "Put her in the peach bedroom. You see she's comfortable and come right back downstairs."

Emory Stokes, arriving next, bussed his hostess, who returned the kiss cordially. "You're looking dapper as usual, Em. I hope you're taking care of yourself."

"I'm feeling fine, my dear," he said. "And you look like a million dollars."

"Not quite that much, I hope. You know how I hate ostentation. Oh, Emory," she whispered as another car pulled up. "You said they weren't coming until tomorrow."

Mrs. Harding gave her most subdued welcome to Alvin Worth, but she made an effort to be gracious with Tikibinitantari. "And Norman and Audrey?" she asked Worth. "Will they be coming this evening?" She had understood that some other engagement would keep Worth and his protegé and both Clawsens busy until lunchtime on Saturday. Alvin Worth could not say when the others would arrive: Norman, he thought, had been called away on some urgent errand. Having nothing else to discuss with him, Bitsy Harding dispatched him to his room. "Come down and have a drink with us after you unpack," she said, hurrying to the kitchen to tell her cook there might be as many as four more for dinner.

George Gresham, intent on keeping his candidacy alive, had arrived early in the afternoon and taken up his position in the living room on the central flagstone of the hearth, able to pivot either to the left, where Bitsy held court from a Napoleon III chaise longue, or to the right, where a cluster of Marvell College ladderback chairs, carved with an *M* and four *V*s of *Vel virtus vel vis,* were grouped for more serious conversations.

Gresham had a well-chosen word to say to each guest as the party assembled. He was assuring Margaret he had long seen an urgent need for a cabinet-level department of education (if he'd supported it prior to its creation, Margaret calculated, he'd sensed the urgency before he left grade school) when Bitsy Harding cut him short: no politics and no political science until after dinner. Her dictum left Emory Stokes in possession of the floor, and Bitsy, conscientious hostess, worked hard to abridge his racy stories for Tiki. She had the air of a responsible mother-for-the-duration-of-your-stay toward an exchange student exceptionally slow to orient himself. She kept it up, simplifying syntax and vocabulary with the speed of a simultaneous interpreter, until the arrival of the Clawsens, Norman preoccupied and Audrey apologetic, presented a greater need.

Tiki, left to himself, could not follow Stokes's tale, a scandalous anecdote about Senate pages, stenographic pools and a hastily gathered quorum for a cloture vote on an all-night filibuster. He wandered over to an elaborate wheeled tea tray on which Inez, the Harding's Peruvian cook, had left large plates of characterful Andean tapas. There he picked up a tube of anchovy paste that the excellent Inez had neglected to tidy away. Tiki squeezed it tentatively, pressing out *pi* and a square root sign. Then, confident the tube worked well enough, he carried it and a handful of canapes over to a malachite coffee table set among the Marvell College chairs. In a few minutes he had written the principal conclusions of Gresham's thesis, all mathematical expressions, in anchovy paste across its gleaming green surface. Firelight flickered over him as he worked: more purposefully and in far less time than he took to set out the equations, he corrected them. By a series of simple operations, executed in contrasting pimiento, he proved them untenable.

Inez, passing round another tray of margaritas, paused in horror, then summoned her mistress.

"What on earth?" Bitsy had not the vaguest idea what it meant, nor had Stokes. The schoolmaster in Inez's village had been shot when she was ten; she only dimly remembered being told that one could not multiply by zero. But she had never known the English words for "zero" or for "multiplication," so she said simply, *"Nada."*

Gresham, who had been laughing uproariously at Stokes's story, repeated *"nada"* softly and froze. Margaret recognized the equations from the last page of Gresham's manuscript, but she had decided, long before reaching the end, that they were irrelevant: his argument was so inane, it wouldn't matter if the math was flawless. Clawsen looked dumbfounded.

Worth, who had done logic before he'd taken up ethics, looked worried and frowned in concentration, his lips moving as he worked through the figures.

"You've made some calculations?" Bitsy said. "Do you need to make a note of them?" She did a little charade, scribbling on her left palm with her right index finger. "Want paper and pencil? Or do you have them here?" she pointed to her head.

"Yes, yes," Tiki smiled and, in turn, pointed to his head. "Here."

"Clean it up, Inez," Bitsy said. "There, just like a slate, wiped clean. All Greek to me!"

"Me too," Emory said.

Worth was still frowning. Gresham had not moved from the table: he could still see the gray and red ciphers on the green stone. He would see them, he thought, for the rest of his life.

"At last!" Bitsy cried theatrically as Bert swept into the room with a radiant young woman on his arm.

"I want you all to meet Susannah Mae," he said. "And let me tell you. What this little lady don't know about the gender gap just ain't worth knowing."

He introduced her first to Margaret, who did not catch her last name, and then to the men, who had leapt to their feet when she entered the room. "Susannah's finishing up a doctorate in political communications at Oral Roberts University," he announced after she had pressed each hand warmly.

Bitsy chose that moment to move the party, still standing, toward the dining room. Bert hesitated before the walnut pocket doors and turned to his wife. "Ladies are a scarce resource tonight, sugar. How are you deploying them?"

The Clawsens' late arrival had occasioned a hurried conference about seating, and he needed to review their fall-back plan. They had intended to put Susannah Mae between Worth and Stokes and across from Margaret, thus communicating directly with three members of the search committee.

Gresham and Tikibooboo were to be isolated, ostensibly in places of honor, Tiki at his hostess's right, George on Bert's left. Now, with another voting member present, Bitsy regrouped: Susannah would be flanked by Worth and Clawsen, facing Stokes, and Margaret placed on Bert's right. Gresham, who did not matter, would remain at Bert's left; Audrey Clawsen, who did not matter either, would buffer Gresham from Stokes. And Bitsy would continue to occupy the enigmatic young Thai. "Inez did place cards, Bert," she said serenely. "People can find their own way."

Audrey Clawsen gasped with wonder as Bert thrust the doors apart. She'd eaten at the Hardings' on other occasions, but never before had they displayed such opulence. The table was laid with Georgian silver—spoons big as ladles, forks large as pitchforks, pistol-grip knives a highwayman might have carried—and delicate French crystal that seemed to shudder in the presence of so much latent violence. In the center of the table, a cascade, no, an avalanche, of orchids tumbled from a golden stand.

"I was just going to put some fruits in the *épergne*," Bitsy Harding was saying to Emory Stokes, "but a friend of ours flew up from Chile yesterday and Bert asked him to bring me a bushel of orchids for Valentine's Day."

"It was on his way." Emory accepted the favor and the splendor as a matter of course. "He had to see Bert before he testified, I suppose."

"I imagine he did. Em, you sit here next to Audrey."

An épergne, Audrey remembered a table-setting from *Town and Country,* that kind of centerpiece was called an épergne and made most likely not of gold but of vermeil. The orchids were arranged in a vermeil épergne, and, because they were Valentine presents, the flowers were pink and red and every shade in between. Audrey's father had always given her mother a big satin heart full of chocolates, but Norman's family had been dirt poor. Both his parents had died young and she'd never met them, but Norman had told her they'd exchanged presents only at Christmas. Thank heavens she was sitting next to Emory, whom she'd known all her life. Her mother always said he was a live wire.

Audrey, glancing down, saw that a cold first course had already been served. She thought it looked like an aquarium. Margaret Donahue, who noticed her distaste, thought the food looked beautiful. It reminded her of a mosaic she'd seen in a book, ancient marine life set forth so realistically that zoologists could identify living species. And Inez, too, had arrayed her specimens with taxonomic nicety: on brilliant aquamarine earthenware plates, she'd set out seven or eight small sea creatures, their natural color only slightly bleached by lime juice, and she'd reproduced a weedy natural habitat for them with shredded ginger, scallions, chilies and coarse sea salt.

"Ceviche?" Susannah smiled knowingly at the voting members who surrounded her. "I've really gotten to love Latino food since I've been in the Southwest."

"Good girl," Bert said.

Norman Clawsen blenched and picked up his fork. The obscene jellylike bodies, the tentacles, the feathery gills revolted him. Tiki prodded the fish curiously with his finger. "Raw," he explained, perhaps to comfort the professor. "Raw, not live."

Margaret speared a squid and gamely bit into it. It was marvelous.

"Do start," Bitsy encouraged her guests. "This is just a little palate teaser to begin."

Norman Clawsen closed his eyes, opened them again, and put down his fork.

"Go ahead, Norm," Bert said. "Don't worry about pollution. These were flown up from South America this morning. They haven't been contaminated by anything worse than guano."

Clawsen murmured his concern about cholesterol, but George Gresham scooped the lot into his soup spoon and swallowed without chewing or inhaling.

"I love new sensations," Susannah announced.

"Then you've come to the right place," Norman Clawsen said.

"That's right," Bert parried the nastiness. "We aren't all stuffy old Yankees at Marvell."

As Audrey Clawsen chewed something she imagined to be a scallop, and really it wasn't too bad, she pondered something truly awful. Norman appeared not to know this Susannah Mae; he seemed, if anything, to dislike her. But had he met her before? He was, after all, the chairman of the search committee.

A blood-red pepper soup, heady and blindingly hot, followed the raw fish. Margaret, who had dined with the committee from time to time, also wondered what was up. Certainly no one with a delicate stomach would be at his best after this meal. When roast boar followed jellied eels, she became more curious still.

Bert carved the boar and, passing a thick slice to Clawsen, asked genially, "You'll be going to merry England this spring, won't you?"

"If my other duties permit, yes. I've been invited to address an international colloquium at one of the newer universities. Most important really, criteria for randomization in voter sampling."

If his other duties permit! What could be more important than their trip to England? Audrey was certain now that her husband was hiding something from her.

"Gentlemen," Bitsy affected to lay down the law. "General conversation at dinner. We're not all political scientists."

"Thank you, my love," Bert raised his glass to his wife. "You keep us civilized."

Forbidden to talk shop, Gresham ate stolidly while Tiki

sampled this dish, as he had the preceding ones, with evident pleasure. Audrey Clawsen said dispiritedly little to Emory Stokes, who made, Margaret thought, every attempt to buck her up. Susannah, animated and girlish, bantered with the table at large, taking care constantly to appeal to Worth and Clawsen.

Inez, at last, cleared the main course and retired to the kitchen, from whence a clatter of copper pots announced the first hitch in a faultlessly served meal. She peeped out of the swinging door and beckoned to Mrs. Harding, who excused herself and flew to join her cook.

"Not to worry," she announced when she rejoined her guests a few minutes later. "Inez couldn't find the salamander."

"Salamander?" Norman Clawsen could not bear much more. He would not have been surprised if chocolate ants appeared as dessert. "Salamander?" he repeated, incredulous.

"It's a kitchen tool, for glazing crème brulée," she explained. "I thought a simple dessert would be nice."

She must eat desserts all the time, Audrey thought. I'd never let myself go like that.

"Why is it called a salamander?" Margaret asked.

"I don't know." Bitsy mulled this over. "Maybe because it has a long handle, like a tail. You heat the body of it over a fire and when it's red hot, you pass it over the sugar to caramelize the crust."

"Maybe," Susannah suggested, "because Aristotle thought salamanders could live in flames."

"Speaking of Aristotle," Alvin Worth began.

"Hush now," Bitsy stopped him. "Here comes Inez with a lovely, rich, unintellectual custard."

Talk did not get technical until after dinner when they moved back into the living room; when it did, Susannah Mae appeared to know more about political polling than Gresham or Tikibinitantari. It had been established during dinner that she knew more about men than Scarlett O'Hara.

Margaret Donahue had long speculated about the differences between men's and women's politics and she was curious about Susannah's dissertation. She rejected the notion that women were more generous or more conciliatory than men, but she'd observed some consistent variations and was disappointed when Susannah Mae said she'd focused on candidate perception and had not, as yet, honed in on issue orientation.

"You actually propose to study sex as an independent variable, Miss, uh, Miss—?" Norman Clawsen asked, coldly skeptical.

"I wish you'd call me Susannah Mae, Professor Clawsen. Gender, not sex."

"Is there a difference?" Bitsy asked. "Have I been missing something all these years?"

"Hush, sugar." Bert laid a hand on his wife's shoulder. "Let her handle this."

"How can you disaggregate . . . ," Gresham objected.

"By regression analysis," she said sharply. "Like with anything else."

"Yes, repression, I mean, regression, that's the ticket." Stokes had never liked Gresham, and Tiki gave him the creeps. This girl was, at the very least, decorative. And there was more money available for women's studies than these turkeys ever dreamed.

"But I do think you're right," she said to appease Clawsen, "that it makes more sense to see gender as a *dependent* variable. I think gender's real interactive."

Audrey Clawsen rose, furious, from the chaise longue on which her hostess had thoughtfully settled her, with a large Cointreau, after dinner. "What I want to know," she said, "is do you review books and attend conventions?"

"Well, I've just begun to," Susannah faltered. "People

rarely ask you, you know, while you're still in graduate school." She could not imagine why this mousy woman was demanding that she be well-connected. Harding's wife was known to be formidable, but nobody had warned her about Mrs. Clawsen.

"Were you in Detroit at Christmastime?" Audrey was white with anger.

"I most certainly was not!" Her emphatic answer sounded like the truth. "I really do not understand why professional meetings are held at such a sacred time, when people ought to be worshiping with their families. I'm beginning to think that Christians are, oh, my gracious—" She'd recalled Marvell was a hotbed of secular humanism. "Well, maybe not a persecuted minority, but, surely to goodness, a *slighted* minority."

"Now, be fair," Bert said. "I don't go to these statistical shindigs myself because they bore me. But I know the plenary sessions didn't start until the twenty-ninth."

"We have eggnog and a big log fire on Twelfth Night," Bitsy explained, "but we don't celebrate continuously."

"You were not in Detroit at all?" Audrey Clawsen took a lot of convincing.

"Not this year. No," Susannah admitted. "If the department feels strongly about it, I suppose I could go in the future."

"Come on, Audrey," Bitsy said. "Let's get a head start on our beauty sleep. I think we can leave Susannah with the elders." Like her mother and her mother-in-law, she taught Sunday School and knew Scripture.

Susannah Mae was not humorlessly devout and acknowledged the joke with a little bubbling laugh. "But, you stay, Miss Donahue. I've been informed"—she smiled in Bert's direction—"that you are the only midcareer fellow who was able to be here this weekend. And you don't need any beauty sleep."

Tiki, who had been straining to understand what had just happened, rushed after the departing ladies. "Missy Clawsen," he shouted. "I net-work too. I have net-worked. I shall net-work."

Saturday breakfast went smoothly, but the afternoon provided a succession of awkward moments that both Hardings passed off as "failures in communication." None of the weekend's drama, however, matched the events of Saturday evening. Shouts and sobs were heard from the Clawsens' room as they changed for dinner. Norman came down alone and announced that Audrey had retired early with a headache. Bitsy took up a stiff lemon juice and bourbon toddy and descended with the cheering news that Audrey would be fine in the morning.

Dinner was served by an expressionless Inez, and conversation became so strained that Bitsy lifted her ban on shoptalk. Susannah seized the opportunity to ask George whether he was descended from the famous Gresham who'd discovered that bad numbers always drive out good numbers, or was it coins. Her question set off a long, snarling debate about the usefulness of mathematical economics between Harding, who said it was bull, and Clawsen and Worth, who said that, within proper parameters, it was true. In most circumstances, their hearers would have preferred silence, but tonight they welcomed an impersonal argument, and while it raged they enjoyed another excellent meal.

Emory Stokes noticeably toyed with his food and excused himself from the table as soon as his hostess had finished her own.

A little later, as Bert led the guests into the living room for liqueurs, the party surprised Emory carrying Audrey across the black and white central hall toward the foot of the staircase. She had fainted, he said, in a gallant attempt to rejoin the party, and he was trying to get her back to her room. That seemed on the face of it unlikely, because she was plainly struggling in his arms and fell limp only as he started to improvise his explanation. Norman Clawsen bolted upstairs after them, and all three left the house before breakfast on Sunday morning.

Sunday was a day of blessed calm. The Hardings took Susannah Mae with them to church, St. John-in-Patmos, Episcopal. Margaret shot pool with Gresham and was pleased to find him a good-natured loser. Alvin Worth showed Tiki the stables and the greenhouses, keeping him, as much as possible, out of doors, but toward evening, Tiki slipped away from Worth and rejoined his host and hostess by the fire. He ran his fingers over the carved back of the Marvell College chairs. *"Vel virtus vel vis,"* he sounded it out curiously. "I do not understand."

"By hook or by crook, son." Bert smiled expansively. "In plain English."

"It is very inspiring," Tiki said and fell silent.

SIXTEEN

JAKE LARSON WAS IMPATIENT, as his plane neared Boston, to see Margaret and to hear about the Hardings' houseparty. Bert had left a resumé in his pigeonhole at the Center before he left. He looked at it now and recognized the candidate's name: she must be the daughter, or perhaps the niece, of a ranking member of the Armed Services Committee, a congressman Harding often invited to the Center. She had gone to a Southern women's college he had never heard of and then to Oral Roberts University. A précis of her dissertation sounded considerably more interesting than Gresham's.

A conniving bunch, he thought, but never dull. Alvin Worth had asked him to lunch at the Faculty Club on the following Wednesday, and Emory Stokes had invited all three labor fellows—Margaret, Lou Stillman and himself—to the symphony and to a Bruins game. He wondered what they'd come up with next. He set Susannah Mae's folder on the tray in front of him and looked out the window at the polar landscape created by the clouds beneath his plane.

His daughter's self-absorbed happiness had not displeased him. Her husband seemed to care for her and to have his wits about him. Living with her mother and stepfather, Karin could have chosen worse. And he had found time, Friday morning when the women in the wedding party were having their hair done, to drop into the city library and photocopy some documents for his labor history paper.

Nonetheless, the wedding itself depressed him. His ex-wife, as mother of the bride, wore a dress with any number of redundant bows, and her habit of referring to her husband, even to their closest friends, as "Dr. Bob," struck him as more rather than less ridiculous with the passage of time. He had been thankful, after placing Karin's hand into her bridegroom's waiting palm, that he could sit by himself. Irene wept noisily against Dr. Bob's tuxedo shoulder throughout the ceremony. "I've always been so vulnerable," he overheard her say to several people on the receiving line, "I'm thankful Karin will be spared the things I had to suffer." He hoped, himself, she'd be spared their wretchedness.

He put the resumé back into his briefcase and took out an obituary he had clipped from the Detroit *Free Press.* It would tickle Margaret after the scene last fall between Lou Stillman and Professor Clawsen. He smiled as he thought of her, plain and fervent. She'd be interested in the documents he'd found, divergent accounts of a famous riot given by strikers and scabs, but he thought she'd find the obituary even more revealing.

Herschel Cohen, a philanthropist of great energy and imagination, had collapsed and died during a dinner given in his honor by the Detroit chapter of the National Conference of Christians and Jews. Mr. Cohen had contributed generously to many causes but above all to neighborhood clinics: ". . . Delivery, that's the problem, the delivery of services. I should know, I was a delivery boy myself," he had just finished saying when he collapsed. Herschel Cohen had left school at the age of fifteen, the article went on to say, working to support his widowed mother, first as a delivery boy, later as a stock clerk, in a grocery store. In time, he built a tristate chain of supermarkets, remarkable for quality and service; he continued till his dying day to visit stores incognito, pinching melons and sniffing the insides of roasting chickens. Although his own formal education ended abruptly, he had kept his younger brothers and sisters in school, and, a modest man himself, bragged joyfully of their achievements. The memorial service had been conducted by his brother, Rabbi Solomon Cohen. In addition to Rabbi Cohen, he was survived by his wife, a son and three daughters, and his sisters—Dr. Rivka Cohen-Levinsky, chief of neonatology at Hadassah Hospital in St. Paul, and Deborah Cohen, an ACLU lawyer in Madison. Surviving also was his youngest brother, Nahum, a professor of politics at Marvell University, who had changed his name legally to Norman Clawsen.

When Larson got back to the Center, he found two notes on his door, both marked Urgent. One requested that he call Margaret, the other that he call Harding.

Margaret answered breathlessly; she must have run to get the phone. "Tom Franchetti has escaped from Bridgewater," she said. "They thought they had him stabilized, and they were moving him out of isolation onto a ward. Donna and her children are here with me."

"Is there a policeman with you now?"

"Yes, Nick Hannibal insisted on it, but he thought it would be better to get them all out of Newnham. He suggested the Sternbergs, but they're away for the weekend."

"There's always Harding. I have a message to call him."

"Why don't you see what he has to say?"

Bert Harding had, in fact, heard about the escape from a stammeringly apologetic warden who knew of his interest in the case from his past, pressing inquiries and advice about security for Franchetti. He'd called Larson to alert him because, so he said, he thought him the most level-headed person staying at the Center. He was leaving for Jakarta within the hour, but he wanted somebody reliable to bring Donna and her daughters to his house immediately. His wife would make sure they had everything they needed.

Larson agreed to drive them out, and that night around midnight, he and Margaret delivered Donna, pale but composed, and two sleepy children into the care of Bitsy Harding, roused to bustling concern for the little girls and vociferous abuse of shrinks.

As they drove back, Margaret regaled him with stories from the Hardings' houseparty. She had nothing but praise for Bitsy Harding's cool head throughout the strained weekend. "And how was your weekend?" she asked, after a painstakingly complete recap.

"I'm glad to be back."

"You MUST UNDERSTAND," Alvin Worth spoke confidentially, as he and Jake drank coffee upstairs in the library after their lunch at the Faculty Club. "Norman's wife is a good woman, utterly devoted to him, but by no means his equal. How could she be?"

"I can't imagine," Jake admitted.

"She cannot sympathize, because she cannot really grasp what his work may mean."

"That's too bad."

"And perhaps inevitably, she lacks training no less than aptitude. The results, however, are more than unfortunate. Some rumor may have reached you of a bizarre scene at the Hardings' houseparty. Mrs. Clawsen constantly importunes Emory Stokes, who, I believe, is an old friend of her family, to find a political post for Norman."

"Does he want to try his hand at politics or government?" The coffee cups were very small and Jake would have been glad for a refill.

"Heaven forfend. Nothing could tempt him less than the

'momentary momentousness of temporary things.' It's an embarrassment to him. And really, I think Emory's more to blame than she is. It flatters him, you see, to be appealed to in that way, it has been decades since he's had any plums to bestow. I can assure you that had he the slightest influence over any appointment, he'd snare it for himself."

"He doesn't strike me, Emory that is, as happy at Marvell."

"He is shallow," Alvin Worth said. "I do not mean that in a pejorative sense."

"No." Jake tried to take another sip from his empty cup.

"He's not deep." Worth changed the subject. "It's unfortunate that you missed the Hardings' party. You miss a good deal, you know, being away so much —the Center's justly famous camaraderie and all . . ."

SEVENTEEN

LARSON HAD BEEN SPENDING most of his weekends in Kentucky since the first attack on UAW organizers there. On the Monday after his lunch with Alvin Worth, he appeared with a bandage on his forehead.

"What happened?" Margaret asked as he sat down beside her before their labor history class. Sam Sternberg was lecturing on constitutional issues raised by the Wagner Act. "There wasn't anything in the papers."

"It's heating up down there," he said. "But this happened in Boston. I left my car in the parking garage at the airport. As I was putting my bag in the trunk, somebody got out of a passing car and slugged me. I chased him, but he hopped onto a shuttle bus and I lost him. The police say there's been a lot of mugging and suitcase snatching."

"Do you think it's just a coincidence?" She was not alarmed, but she was suspicious.

"Probably," he said. "I'll park in a more exposed spot next time."

"I'll meet you," she said.

"What sort of relations are there between the patrolmen's union and the Teamsters?" he asked.

"Not as cool as they ought to be," she said. "Both the metropolitan police and the state police cover the airport.

The jurisdictions overlap, but the locals are quite autonomous." She brushed his hair back, to get a better look at the bandage. "I'll meet your plane next Sunday," she repeated. "I don't like this. It sounds funny."

"Okay," he said. "I'll take your word for it. You know Boston, but be careful."

" 'I am a Union Maid,' " she said. " 'I never am afraid of goons and ginks—' "

" '—and company finks,' " he finished. "I know you're not afraid. But don't take any chances."

THE NEXT SUNDAY Margaret drove to Logan Airport an hour before Jake's plane was due. The flight was scheduled to arrive at ten, and throughout the day young persons employed by Piedmont Airlines maintained with implacable optimism that the flight would be on time. Margaret wanted to circle the floors of the multistoried parking garage well in advance of the arrival time and continue to monitor it throughout the evening. She drove systematically up and down the ramps, thinking how easy it would be, simply by telephone, to shadow someone flying from one city to another. The airline would confirm departure. Anyone else, a ticket clerk or a coffeeshop busboy, could make sure the person had boarded. And where could someone more plausibly loiter than in an airport? Nothing was more commonplace than delays or missed flights. Nothing, perhaps, save this circling of the garage, looking for a parking place on the weekend.

She saw a man, hard-faced and somewhat more shabbily dressed than was customary for air travelers, standing on the landing of a staircase; another, a little too well-dressed for auto repair, tinkered under the hood of his car. On the roof, a young man flagged her down and said he'd left his parking lights on. Could she give him a jump start? She said she didn't have cables but promised to send help. The state trooper she notified told her she'd been smart not to get out of her car; he'd have a tow truck sent up, but he doubted the car would still be there. There'd been a couple of rapes that month.

The night got darker, and the garage eerier. The poured concrete ceiling glowed above orange sodium globes. Its surface neither absorbed nor reflected their light, merely suffered it, leaving the shadows beneath untouched. Chiaroscuro, Margaret thought, it's really terrifying when nothing exists in moderation and everything's utterly naked or pitch-black. She noted the starkness of the stairwells, lit almost lemon yellow with another sort of bulb, the railings' painted and peeling black enamel. She felt herself seized with horror, scarcely able to breathe. She grabbed the steering wheel hard and shook herself impatiently.

When she finally entered the terminal, she felt herself again, ashamed by her fears, brusque and competent. She inquired about the 9:58 due in from Louisville and was again assured the plane would be on time. She bought coffee and sat down with Emma Goldman's autobiography, closing the book after reading what Emma had to say about the beatings her lover endured at the hands of Pinkertons and company goons. She wished Jake would simply call for a jurisdictional election and let the National Labor Relations Board take it from there, but he was a pro. There'd be no election until he knew he had the votes to win it.

At 9:50 she made her way toward Gate Five. The plane had not landed; a few others were waiting. A young man with carnations wrapped in cellophane, some women in sweaters and slacks, one elegantly dressed, pacing and smoking. A routine delay. Margaret sat down in the waiting area and tried to read, but her eyes refused to focus on the page. Instead she saw famous massacres: Haymarket, Homestead, River Rouge.

She saw strikers fall, beaten and bloodied. "I am a Union Maid. I never am a—frayed . . ."

"Husband late, ma'am?" The man spoke musically, Cuban she thought.

"No," she almost shouted. The smiling brown-skinned man was wiping the floor; she lifted her feet automatically so he could clean underneath her chair.

"Husband plane late?" he repeated, wringing out his mop and working carefully around her.

"No," she said. "I'm waiting for someone I work with."

The plane landed an hour and a half later. Travelers emerged and paired themselves with the people waiting for them. There was no sign of Jake. At last Margaret rose reluctantly to her feet, wondering whom to call in Louisville. She knew Jake stayed in a motel, but he'd never mentioned its name. She thought she would not call a newspaper, not yet at any rate. It was now past midnight. She'd just resolved to call the local head of the American Federation of Teachers, whom she knew slightly, when Larson appeared. He strode through the passenger gate, and she ran forward, tripped and almost fell into his arms. "So stupid of me. I was up all night Saturday. I fell asleep on the flight. They had a devil of a time waking me up so they could vacuum my seat."

"It doesn't matter," she said again and again.

"I'm lucky I'm not on my way to Rochester. Hey," he said, seeing tears in her eyes, "you never are afraid, remember?"

"I wasn't afraid," she said. "I was furious."

The man with the mop reappeared. "Husband come?"

"I think he's Hispanic," Margaret explained. "I couldn't make him understand you were my colleague."

"I'm here," Larson said, in good Spanish, holding out his hand to the man. "Thanks for keeping my friend company while she waited for me." They exchanged pleasantries for a few minutes, and the man went off down the corridor with a cheery wave.

"Your political instincts are good," she said.

"I like people."

"Do you have luggage?"

"Only carry-on," he said. "Let's go."

The trooper she'd spoken with earlier approached them. "I'm glad to find you, ma'am. That blue Pontiac you reported stalled on the roof. It was gone when the truck got there."

"As you predicted."

"Yes, can you give me a description of the man you saw?"

As they drove away from the airport, a pistachio green Cadillac Fleetwood cut sharply into Margaret's lane. She swerved to avoid it, accelerated to get a look at the driver, then laughed when she saw the couple in the front seat: a balding man and a woman about the same age who still wore the lacquered beehive hairdo of her youth. Not in the least sinister. Their car sported two bumper stickers: BUSH/QUAYLE '88 and the intertwined rings of Marriage Encounter Workshops.

"It's funny," she said, "to think of that pair spending a weekend in a Holiday Inn massaging each other under the approving eyes of the clergyman of their choice." Her sister and brother-in-law did that from time to time, so she was well-informed about the group's practices.

"It's not such a bad idea. It's good for couples to get away sometimes." He spoke quietly and she thought he sounded tired. "Margaret, would you spend next weekend with me?"

"I'd love to see the plant." She had wanted to go to Kentucky since he first told her about the trouble there, but she'd never asked, fearing she'd be in his way. "It has a new sort of assembly line, doesn't it? That allows for task rotation?"

"I'd be happy to show it to you, but I was thinking about driving up to Vermont. We could see the maple-sugaring."

"Jake, are you asking me to spend the weekend with you as in, as in . . . ?" She found she did not know what to call it.

"Yes. I want to be alone with you."

She was so stunned she said not another word until they reached the Center, and then Jake, who never spoke unnecessarily, said, "Come up for a drink."

"Okay." She was sleepwalking.

When they got to his rooms, he took her coat and poured her a shot of bourbon. "Margaret, we know each other well and we like each other a lot."

"We do. Yes," she began hesitantly, taking her accustomed place on the couch. "Yes, I do like you a lot. A lot."

"And, now, now I'm the one who wants more. Don't you too?"

"I don't know." She really did not know what to say or think or do. "I don't know." She was staggered and thoroughly perplexed. She set her drink down in order to concentrate. Her thoughts were so scattered that holding a glass distracted her.

"That's a first." He was sitting across the room in the chair where he usually sat when they studied together. "You're generally pretty decisive." He made no move toward her; apparently he was prepared to discuss this rationally. Was that why these gambits were called 'propositions'?

"I don't know what to say. I care a great deal about you. I hadn't realized how much. But . . ." She was trying to be rational too. "But, sex . . ."

"Margaret," it dawned on him. "Are you a virgin?"

"I'm a forty-seven-year-old Irish spinster. Of course I'm a virgin."

"What about your Young Republican? Didn't he try to make love to you?"

That was her bitterest memory, by far the worst. She had never told anyone about it. Not even her sister, Nora, whom she might have told at the time. She had wondered, when Nora began dating Jim Clancy herself, whether she would be willing to sleep with him before they were married. Nora was a regular communicant but a pragmatist.

"He must have tried, if he was such a sleazy eager beaver."

"He did. And I wouldn't. I was terrified of getting pregnant."

"You were a respectable girl."

"Yes. And he said . . ." She wanted to tell Jake, but she could barely get the words out even now. "This former altar boy, this defender of the faith, said to me, 'I thought all you pinkos believed in free love.'"

"What a jerk."

"He was a jerk. I'd have respected him if he believed in free love himself, or if he'd really believed in chastity. You must have heard that nuns used to tell kids premarital sex was a mortal sin. One of the psychopaths who lurked in lovers' lanes could kill you right after you did it, and you'd go straight to hell. He didn't believe that—that some ax-murderer would crawl into the back of his Ford and kill us—any more than he really thought Khrushchev had designs on Alaska."

"So it wasn't just politics and social mobility you fought about?" he asked.

"We fought about a lot of things, but basically it was always the same fight."

"You really are very pure."

"I don't know about that. But I haven't been a novice at anything for a long time. I can't start now." She looked painfully embarrassed.

He crossed the room and sat down next to her. "Margaret, lovemaking isn't an Olympic event. It's crazy to think about being new at it, or good at it."

She considered this. "I guess you're right. If it were so very difficult, we'd be extinct. Anybody must be able to . . ."

"Not just anybody, Margaret," he said encouragingly. "You."

"How do you know?"

"Because I already know you so well. Sex—" he expounded

lucidly, facing her—"sex is like collective bargaining, a lot of preliminary protestation and coaxing and stroking . . ."

"And then?" That seemed at once a novel and a manageable prospect.

"Then, you try to stay fairly calm until you sense that losing your composure will have the maximum effect. You must have done it hundreds of times."

"I have," she said.

"Okay?"

"Jake," she said. "It scares me."

"Think it over. You don't have to decide tonight."

"I'm frightened. Please hold me." She was shaking. "Tighter. You asked me if I loved him. I didn't. I never loved any man except . . ."

"Who, Margaret?" Larson was accustomed to putting himself in other people's shoes and his thoughts raced. Who was it Margaret loved? The streetwise gym teacher, the exmarine she'd worked with to expel Franchetti? The guy must be married. Somebody in the state federation? A sincerely Catholic colleague, who loved her, too, but wouldn't divorce? With several children, very likely, so apart from his scruples, he could barely support one family on his lousy salary . . . "Who, Margaret? Tell me." The pain in his voice broke her down.

"My father." She wept harshly, choking on her words. "He was the only man I ever knew who really cared about the things I cared about. Whether people were treated decently, whether the pictures they looked at were ugly or beautiful, whether the things preached at them were lies or not lies."

As her sobbing subsided, she felt Jake's collarbone underneath his shirt and she began to think about his body, about the articulation of his bones. Would all the joints in his body be strong and awkward and pleasing to her, like his hands and wrists and jaw? "I don't want to wait until next weekend," she said.

"Margaret, you're distraught. I hadn't realized how this would affect you."

"Please."

"I want to very much. Believe me. But you're very tense now."

"Jake, you're stalling."

"All right." He walked to the window and opened it wide. Cold, fresh air filled the room, and he leaned out and found Orion among the dim city stars. Winter was almost over: one more bound would carry the hunter beyond the western horizon. "All right," he repeated, turning back to her. "Margaret, I'll take this very slow."

A SOFT TAP ON THE OUTER DOOR of the suite wakened Jake shortly before dawn.

"The ax murderer," he said. "Right on cue."

EIGHTEEN

THE SKY OVER FLORENCE had been gray for days, dove gray; the city's narrow streets and narrower sidewalks, slate gray. Rain filled the Arno and the river darted like quicksilver, a fluid, shining gray. Rain continued to fall, silvery too and plummet-straight. Molly marveled that there could be so much dampness without mist or fog. The buildings kept their acute edges. Their splendid shapes looked as they always did, as if a sure hand had drawn them in seconds, without hesitation, with perfect certainty: there were no gargoyles lurking here, and no enshrouding fog.

Molly loved walking through the city each morning to the library. Today the elderly *servitore* who opened the door greeted her excitedly. Like many who held sinecures in French and Italian archives, he had fought with the partisans: first making history, then watching over it. She heard his stories with pleasure, and he had told her many times that it pleased him she was marrying a man of action. Her fiancé had called a few minutes before on a matter of great urgency, he said, adding that he spoke Italian well.

"Nothing the matter?"

"Have no fear. His voice was firm. Perhaps he has been shot, but he will recover. I can hear these things, even over a wire."

Molly placed the call, trembling, not wholly reassured by the old man's experience. Nick's voice did calm her. He was clearly all right. "Molly, I think you ought to get here as soon as you can. There's been a murder at the Center."

"Not Sam?"

"No, Jake Larson, you remember him?"

"Of course, Margaret's friend. That's dreadful."

"Margaret's lover, Molly."

"Nick, is this one of your famous hunches?"

"No, it isn't. And so far, she's been fine. She called a doctor instantly and then called me. But she remembers nothing before hearing a shot and finding him nearly dead."

"Nick, Margaret *told* you they were lovers?" Molly found this almost incredible. In her experience, people never fell in love unless they were able to suspend disbelief. Margaret impressed her as supremely disabused and, Molly judged, far too fastidious for casual sex.

"She's forthright about everything she can remember."

"They weren't lovers at Christmas, were they?"

"It never crossed my mind. I wouldn't have said so."

"How is she?"

"She's holding herself together, but she's fragile."

"I can get an evening flight out of Milan." I may not be her closest friend, Molly thought, and she may not want to talk about it with anyone, but she ought to know people care enough about her to be there if she does want them. "Don't tell her I'm coming. She'd never hear of my leaving my work. I'll just turn up."

MARGARET WALKED AIMLESSLY through Newnham. Jake had been dead for a day, and this morning, the first without him, dawned warm and moist. She was unprepared to find the spring so far advanced. It seemed she had been indoors for weeks while, around the city's gentrified houses, waves of blue scilla beat back the receding snow; everywhere, bulbs thrust themselves through leaves abandoned the previous fall. One green stalk, she saw, had pierced a maple leaf and lifted it inches above the ground. The flowers' assertive beauty contrasted oddly with the stolid ugliness of the houses shingled, or vinyl-sided, in drab pastels. Under a different sky, Margaret reflected, you'd think the sun had drained those wan colors of a life they once possessed; here, you knew they'd never lived at all.

But far uglier than the triple deckers, she thought, were their ornaments. The decorative impulse broke out in Newnham in an extravagance of kitsch she had never seen equaled: lurid birds, parrots, seagulls, bluejays and cardinals, made of jewel-toned plastic leaded like stained-glass, hung in bay windows. Here and there, mylar butterflies, poised on suction cups, quivered among the birds; beneath them, on the window sills, were milkglass baskets full of artificial flowers and single red silk roses, sold by Mass Citizens for Life, set in plastic bud vases pressed to imitate cut crystal.

She passed a school, its windows no better than the houses', trimmed predictably in February with hearts, each red and perfectly symmetrical. Margaret had struggled to bring a measure of invention and unpredictability to elementary school art, but month after month, year after year, teachers issued construction paper in one color, the seasonal color only, and decreed turkeys and pilgrim hats at Thanksgiving, trees at Christmas, hearts, shamrocks, tulips, rabbits and flags as the school year drew to a close. She cut through the playground of the school and turned again toward home, feeling hot and weak. She unbuttoned her coat, pulled the scarf from her neck and took a deep breath of the languorous air.

Margaret's own neighborhood had resisted gentrification, and as she got closer to home, more and more figures cluttered the front yards. They multiply at night, she thought: plastic Santas with sleighs and reindeer, plastic creches put up in November, left in place until Easter. Plaster-of-paris ducks, donkeys, gnomes and cupids; birdbaths, sacred and secular, served as pedestals either to St. Francis or a nymph. Saints she did not recognize with attributes she found hard to reconcile. And everywhere, the Virgin Mary. The Blessed Mother appeared in molded plaster grottoes, some smooth, some scalloped. Mary Immaculate. Margaret wished she could remember the night she had spent with Jake. It seemed so cruel to have lost him and that memory of him all at once.

Statues of Mary were often swathed in plastic sheeting to protect them from the winter weather. Margaret paused before one, all but invisible behind a bevy of flamingos, painstakingly wrapped in an old shower curtain and lashed with clothesline. A young woman standing on the porch of the house followed Margaret's gaze. "I think it's safe to unwrap her, don't you?" She had been Margaret's student years before; now she was her neighbor and still turned to her for advice.

"I think so."

"The air's so gorgeous today," she said as she untied the knots and lovingly unveiled the figure. "She'd want to feel it against her cheek. I mean," she seemed uncertain the schoolteacher would follow her, "I mean, if it was really Her."

"Anyone would."

"You're taking courses at Marvell now, aren't you? Did you know the man who was murdered?"

"Yes."

"That's too bad." She rolled the clothesline into a tight ball and set it down at her feet. "The *Herald* didn't say anything about his family. Usually they do."

"He was divorced, with a married daughter."

"It could be worse, then, I guess. It's sad, though, dying so sudden." She shook out the shower curtain and folded it deftly. "I can wrap her up again if they predict a storm."

"You do a neat job of it, Patty," Margaret said.

"Thanks, Miss Donahue." She was seldom praised these days and Margaret's words recalled happier days. "My parents put it up the spring I was May Queen. I gotta go in now and make Billy's lunch. See you later, Miss Donahue."

Something about the statue caught Margaret's eye. As always, Mary's foot was set down daintily on the serpent's head. That lack of decision had puzzled Margaret throughout her childhood: if Evil incarnate slithered underfoot, why not crush it while you had the chance? But today, the object in the snake's mouth arrested her.

It appeared to be a rose. She leaned over the fence and stared. Had the serpent seized a flower? No, paint flaking off the apple gave the illusion of petals. How strange!

Margaret's street, named perversely after a minor Puritan divine, was rich in statuary and she passed three Sacred Hearts. Red and gold against immaculate white tunics, conventional as valentines, they looked nothing at all like the chaos of blood and muscle, splintered bone and scorched skin that she never ceased to see. Everything was perfectly clear from the moment she first saw Jake fallen back across the threshold of his room; she rehearsed the day's events again and again, hoping to get back beyond that image.

First she had phoned for help, then she knelt next to Jake, attempting to stanch the bleeding with a towel, but never doubting the wound would be fatal. She spoke his name over and over, but he had never answered, nor, she supposed, ever heard. When she'd taken up his hand, he hadn't pressed hers in recognition, and she had never been able to find a pulse. A doctor and an emergency squad, dispatched from the teaching hospital connected with Marvell's medical school, got there within a quarter of an hour of her call and, as promptly, pronounced him dead. They found her calm, clearheaded, in street clothes. Having nothing else with her, she had dressed hastily, crouching close to Jake's body as she waited for them.

Nick, arriving shortly after the medical team, had questioned her gently, and Margaret, dismayed that she remembered so little, had been surprised he found no fault with her vagueness. She repeatedly apologized, and he, as often, reassured her, "Margaret, even eyewitnesses never give a complete account. Things happen too fast. Perception and memory are too selective. You know that. Ask three different people what happened at a meeting. Go home and lie down. Try to clear your mind and then tell me what comes. Don't force connections."

As soon as she'd gotten home yesterday morning, she'd realized she omitted something. Nick hadn't asked what she was doing there at daybreak: he must have assumed she'd had some academic reason to stay overnight. Jake had fallen in such a way that the door couldn't be closed without moving his body, so nobody needed to ask her how she'd gotten into the room. Margaret had tried several times during the day and early evening to reach Nick and eventually he had called her. "I just got the message you called. It's been pandemonium here. There was a double murder in the South End . . ."

Conscious of a duty to withhold no fact, she had blurted it out—certain her illicit passion would seem ludicrous to him —that she'd gone to bed with Jake the night before he was killed. Nick, she recalled gratefully, had sprung forward with ready sympathy. "Margaret, why didn't you say so? Shall I come over or would you rather be alone?"

"I guess there are some things I should tell you. I can come down to headquarters."

"At eleven at night? Don't be ridiculous. I'm on my way."

He had arrived with bread, cheese and an excellent antipasto prepared for take out by an upscale pizzeria. "You and

Molly always provide good food at a wake," she said. "Very thoughtful."

"You haven't eaten today, have you?"

"No," she admitted.

He had cut some bread and cheese and handed her a plate of pickled eggplant and peppers.

"I'm sure I spent at least part of the night with him, but what I told you this morning remains the truth as far as I know it. I have no memory of anything before the shot. I'm certain I was naked when I first saw him lying there. He'd put on a robe, probably to answer the door. I don't remember a phone call or a knock on the door or any conversation." She paused; she could summon up nothing but a total and terrifying blankness. "Nick, I didn't shoot him, did I?"

"Of course not. Where would you have found a gun?"

"I don't know. Maybe he had a gun. Maybe I blanked that out too. God knows what I might have done. Irish women are so repressed."

He heard a note of hysteria in her voice and dashed it coldly. "Yes, I know. That's why I avoid them."

"Sorry," she said.

"Come on, Margaret. You're left-handed, aren't you, and close to Larson's height?"

"As simple as that?"

"Simple to rule you out. Less simple to find a right-handed person shorter than Larson who could get into and out of the Center with a gun, or who'd be able to hide a weapon there. Who'd want to kill Jake, Margaret?"

"Goons," she said and described the struggle between the two unions in Kentucky. "I dreamt of some sort of fracas every time he went down there."

"Did he ever say anything to you about having a gun or getting a gun?"

"No, never."

"But he had been attacked, hadn't he? Do you know how he got that gash on his forehead?"

"In Boston at the airport, a week ago. That's why I met his plane last night."

"Did you see anything suspicious at Logan?"

"Several things." She found all that easy to remember: the janitor, the people watching in the parking garage or waiting in the terminal, even the name and badge number of the state trooper who'd taken such a long time to get back to her.

Nick had listened thoughtfully and asked many questions, but when she'd exhausted her recollections, he'd wanted to talk about the Center, about Jake's relations with people at Marvell.

"Jake got along with everybody at the Center. He was the most easygoing man I've ever known who wasn't a fool himself."

Nick knew what she meant. He was occasionally rougher on people than he ought to be.

"Alvin Worth seemed to be cultivating Jake. They had lunch together a couple of times. Jake told me they mostly talked about George Gresham. Worth said that a layman might not understand how progressive Gresham really was, that the policy implications of his work weren't readily apparent but that he'd always been a staunch friend of organized labor."

"That sounds pretty feeble."

"And insulting. They were supposed to be looking for a scholar, not a speech writer." She was crumbling a piece of crisp bread in her fingers.

"What about Harding?"

"The only argument they ever had was about the Teamsters. Bert took up union corruption a few years ago and wrote an article people are still talking about. He argued that democratic unions were less effective. In general the corrupt ones, like the Teamsters, did better by their members."

"And Jake disagreed, I imagine."

"Vehemently. He said it was criminal to make that argument respectable and that it was simply wrong on the merits. Challenges to authority kept it smart as well as honest. Bert finally said Jake had a point. He could think of lots of brains that tenure had turned to mush."

"I'm so sorry, Margaret." She couldn't have found many people who rang as true to her as Jake had.

"Tom Franchetti drives a truck, you remember," Margaret said. "When he's sober enough to show up."

"I know. What do Harding's colleagues think about him?"

"Clawsen and Worth cast suspicion on Bert at every opportunity, mostly in connection with Donna."

"Margaret," Nick broached this gently, "the night we all had dinner after Dick Llewellyn was killed, Jake told us he'd had a run-in with Tommy."

"And I was upset he hadn't mentioned it to me."

"Shall I make some coffee? Where do you keep it?"

"No, thanks. Tommy was irrationally jealous of everyone. Was he rationally jealous of Jake, is that what you're wondering?"

He nodded and she said, "Do you know, I really haven't the least idea? I never thought about Jake and women. I knew he was divorced. I wondered how they'd broken up, but I never wondered if he was sleeping with somebody. He didn't seem attached to anyone and I've no idea if, well, if he did it recreationally. I don't think he'd do anything irresponsible."

"I'd trust your instincts about that. I'm frankly stymied about Dick Llewellyn's murder too, but I can't believe they're not connected. Can you think of anything else?"

"The Center's a snake pit. Alvin Worth really seems to hate Stokes. Stokes was very attentive to Clawsen's wife at the Hardings' house party, but Worth seems to be the one who resents it. Jake saw Worth and Stokes quarreling in the hall outside Worth's office the Monday morning after the party."

"Will you be able to sleep?" he'd asked when they'd run out of things to talk about.

"I'm very tired now."

"Okay. I'll let you get some rest. Call me if I can help with anything. Call me anytime."

She had fallen asleep after he left, woke early and restless, and immediately set forth on this walk. It had helped her, she realized as she returned to the undistinguished brick building where she lived, to talk with Nick last night about the whodunit aspects. Thinking of Jake, alive or dead, would be, for some time, too much for her. Her building had an elevator, but she preferred to take the stairs four flights up to her small, modern apartment where she was distracted as little as possible by housekeeping details. She brewed a pot of black tea—she kept loose tea in her kitchen, but little else that required much thought—and took it, with a pear, into the living room.

NINETEEN

"LIEUTENANT HANNIBAL, I have been eager to assist your inquiry. As you well know, I have volunteered information. But this is appalling." Alvin Worth felt more than aggrieved, he felt violated. He waited, with tightly drawn lips, as a uniformed policeman opened the door to his office. "I suppose you have a warrant?"

"Yes, I have." Nick Hannibal took the document from his breast pocket and handed it to the professor. "Thanks, Bill, you can wait out here," he said to the man who stood guard and, stepping aside, let Worth go in first. "I know it's inconvenient to be kept out of your office and a nuisance to have it searched, but the president has asked for everyone's cooperation."

"Good heavens, has Bert dragged *him* into this? Bertram Harding has no discretion, no sense at all of what he owes the university."

"Excuse me, I meant the president of Marvell. I should have made that clear." The dean of the Center, Caleb Tuttle, was abroad, unreachable in the Carpathian mountains. In his absence, Nick had met with Marvell's president Manley Trimmer, and it proved a useful meeting. Affable and well briefed, Trimmer had ridden out several scandals, so he recognized those that, like homicide, he could not finesse. "Mr. Trimmer agreed to a complete search of the Center."

"Very well, then, but I am afraid this case is very simple," Worth said as he opened the drawers of his desk and presented their contents for inspection with exaggerated courtesy. Everything was carefully arranged: stacks of writing paper—large and small—notecards in several colors, handsome commemorative stamps, red and black ink cartridges. No clutter, nothing out of place, and, as Nick expected, no gun, no ammunition, no hint that anything of the kind had ever been there.

"Thank you," he said. "And now, the safe. I think each office has one."

Worth removed his boots and stood in his stocking feet on a chair to reach the fine drypoint engraving of Kant that concealed the door of his wall safe. "It seems childishly simple to me. Franchetti's still at large. You've been unable to locate him, and that's more than unfortunate considering . . ." The safe did not open the first time he tried the combination: his hand was shaking, Nick noticed, and he stopped talking to collect himself.

"I agree." Franchetti had been seen briefly in Newnham after escaping from the hospital, but—a hitherto unimpeachable source in the Limerick bar told Nick—he'd learned that his girlfriend was pregnant and taken flight, her father in hot pursuit. Eluding due process while risking family vengeance, Nick thought—as if anyone needed further proof that he was crazy. "Extremely unfortunate."

"Eventually, I trust, he'll be returned to custody and his troubles diagnosed. In the meantime, we at the Center will be demeaned, some of us perhaps irreparably." Worth stepped down from the chair and heaped his desk with papers from the safe. "Take them with you, if you like. I don't think you'll learn very much from them."

"I'm looking for a murder weapon," Nick said. "I've no wish to read private papers."

"These are by no means private. They've been only too

thoroughly reviewed." He handed Nick a score of typewritten articles, accompanied by withering commentary and perfunctory letters of rejection from scholarly journals; the more encouraging notes proposed major revisions or, as the topmost letter read, "in-depth reconceptualization."

A yellow envelope, emptied of the photographs it once contained, fell out from among the papers, a thin film of color negative slipping out of it to the floor. Nick stooped to retrieve it. "Go ahead," Worth taunted him, "you might as well know all there is to know about the Center. Have a look."

Nick took the negatives to the window and saw on them pictures of Emory Stokes with a woman he did not recognize. They were seated on a park bench, apparently deep in conversation. In one frame her hand was laid upon his sleeve, in another he was wiping her eyes with a handkerchief. The entire sequence seemed so innocuous Nick thought Worth must be joking. "These would be worth millions, if you weren't an honest man." He smiled, handing them back to Worth. "I'm sorry to have taken so much of your time."

"You don't understand," Worth said, affronted. "The woman is the wife of a colleague, Norman Clawsen's wife, Audrey. I would do anything to prevent their circulation."

Anything except destroy them, Nick thought. "Women occasionally confide in men other than their husbands. Surely these photographs are not compromising . . ." He waited for Worth to explain.

"Your profession may acquaint you with a wider variety of women than does mine." Worth was not, at the moment, prepared to say more.

Most investigations revealed petty secrets, sad or squalid and irrelevant to the crime; Nick accepted this, and he hadn't supposed Marvell's faculty would bear the indignities any better than most people. This office-to-office search, however distasteful, was necessary: the murder weapon almost certainly remained within the sprawling complex that housed all the Center's activities. The building was locked each night at midnight. It had the requisite number of fire exits, but none of them could be opened without setting off an alarm, and the alarm system, tested periodically during the night by a watchman walking rounds, had been in perfect order on the night of the murder. Fellows and faculty members had keys to the main door, but this, the only nighttime entrance, was equipped, like all other exits, with metal detectors. It was kept, day and night, under video surveillance, and the tape revealed no one leaving or entering from the time, around one A.M., when Larson and Margaret had come in together until the night watchman let in the medical team at 6:25 that morning.

It seemed unlikely the killer had let himself out a window. The lower floors, impenetrable and climate-controlled, had no windows that could be opened. Offices above the third floor had working windows because Caleb Tuttle refused to accept the deanship unless promised fresh air. Someone might have jumped or lowered himself from an upper window. It would be a dangerous jump, though hardly life-threatening, particularly if a person knew how to land, but Nick believed it hadn't been attempted. The heavy January snows had been eroded by successive thaws and cold snaps: the snow shrank and crusted until it looked and felt like styrofoam. It would bear no weight. All around the Center, the verge of snow that lay between its outer wall and the shoveled paths gave no sign that any heavy object, let alone a falling body, had broken through its brittle surface.

Norman Clawsen was writing feverishly at a library table when Nick approached him. "I have to lecture in twenty minutes."

"I can come back whenever it's convenient."

"Never mind." Clawsen counted the sheets of paper. "I

have enough to get me through an hour. I'll accompany you to my office and then I'll give you a free hand."

Yet he lingered as Nick examined his bookshelves and his desk, padding back and forth in carpet slippers. His snow boots, identical to Worth's, were set neatly on yesterday's newspaper outside his office door. He made nervous conversation, lamenting Larson's death, speculating on the connection between his murder and Llewellyn's and, at last, resuming the lecture on social science method begun at the Sternbergs' party. "There's just one killer, I imagine. Principle of parsimony, perhaps you have encountered the idea before—the best, the most scientifically elegant explanation is always the simplest."

"The simplest that can accommodate all the facts. And murder's usually lavish with awkward facts. Now, if I could see the safe . . ."

"Explanation demands simplification."

"But not oversimplification. The safe, sir?" Nick wondered as he cut him short if that had been a mistake. What would he have to say about his colleagues if left to speculate unchecked?

With manifest reluctance, Clawsen took down from his office wall a well-framed photograph of himself, a decade or so younger, accepting an award for the nontenured scholar who had in the last twelve months most advanced the discipline of political science. The award itself, in a silverplated frame, hung beside the pale rectangle in which the door of Clawsen's safe stood exposed.

"Lieutenant Hannibal, would it not suffice if I gave you my word that this safe contains nothing but books and papers?"

"Mr. Trimmer thought," Nick answered obliquely, "a thorough search would restore everyone's confidence. The Center has been shaken by these killings, and he wants its work to go forward."

"It's crucial, of course," Clawsen acknowledged, bowing

his head, in submission or reverence, "that nothing jeopardize our collective endeavor. Very well then, if I must, I must. I have been married for many years," he added pleadingly, as he turned to work the combination.

That statement usually served to introduce a banal confession. Nick was prepared to hear it and disregard it. Perhaps this was the reason Mrs. Clawsen wept in the company of another man. But adultery was not Clawsen's weakness: his safe contained many back issues of *Cosmopolitan* and a number of the most rudimentary sex manuals, nothing that could not be bought in any of a dozen book shops within five blocks of the Center. Nick looked through the books to assure himself that, anodyne as they appeared, they had not been hollowed out to conceal something else. They were what they appeared. Sophomoric. None would have rated more than a smirk in a junior high school locker room, but they seemed to have been bought in distant cities. Their bookmarks advertised discount booksellers in Berkeley, Ann Arbor and Chapel Hill. All were annotated, and several were highlighted with yellow fluorescent pen.

"Thank you," Nick said, "I'm sorry I interrupted you."

Sam's safe, Nick thought as he made his way to Sternberg's office, would be a welcome relief. Sam cheerfully took from his safe and set out on his desk a list of questions prepared in advance for spring term exams so he could get away early for a symposium on municipal autonomy in the West Bank, a black three-ring notebook full of working papers for that conference—several highly detailed and profoundly damaging to their authors were they circulated prematurely—and an angel-skin coral necklace, Miranda's birthday present. ("She refuses to wear precious stones," Sam explained, in defense of the beads, which, Nick thought, required no extenuation.) "And this last," Sam said, removing a sealed envelope, "is a painful case."

"What is it?"

"An article submitted to the *Law Review,* transparently plagiarized. Half is cribbed from one of Felix Frankfurter's most famous dissents; the other half, less famous but familiar enough, I wrote myself when I clerked for Justice Brennan. The boy who claims to have written it hates law school. He wants to be a filmmaker, but he suffers from an insane divorced mother in Bayonne, New Jersey, whose last hope for earthly glory he represents."

"What are you going to do?"

"Confront him with it and tell him to withdraw."

"That sounds like what he wants."

"It's a little better than he deserves. He's my friend Lou Stillman's nephew, but that's not the reason I haven't reported him. The disciplinary apparatus here is run by failed academics and aging preppies preserved in alcohol. A lot of them haven't lived outside a dormitory since they were first sent to boarding school. They aren't bad people, but their experience of the world is pitifully limited. The faculty should accept responsibility ourselves for judging cases like this, but nobody has the time."

That was a long speech for Sam, and more alienated from Marvell than he usually sounded.

"What's the article about, Sam?"

"About legal questions that arise when two unions are trying to organize the same workforce."

"Jake Larson was involved in exactly that."

"I know. And he'd discussed it at length with Lou. But they were more concerned with political than legal problems, and neither of them knew about this article. The editor of the *Law Review,* on the other hand, is a fledgling legal eagle. She recognized the sources as soon as she saw it and brought it straight to me."

"I'll have to make sure."

"Sure. You don't really expect to find the murder weapon in the Center, do you?"

"I don't think it could have been removed after the murder. Could Larson himself have had a gun? I understand there'd been troubles in Kentucky."

"It would have been very contrary to policy if he had. He was a rising star, slated for a vice-presidency in the UAW. They're not a gun-toting crew."

"What about your colleagues then?"

"Bert Harding's celebrated gun collection, you'll soon see if you haven't already, is chiefly ornamental."

"Apart from Harding, who knows about guns? Could anyone break a gun down and clean it thoroughly, so you couldn't tell how recently it'd been fired?"

"I doubt it. I don't think Bert himself would know how. Caleb Tuttle's the last of the heroic generation. He spent four years underground in Eastern Europe where he's traveling now."

"He might have kept whatever gun he carried then," Nick suggested.

"He probably did. I've left messages for him in Budapest and in Prague. I'll ask him when he calls in."

"It wouldn't be hard to get into his office?" Nick had noticed that however impressive the Center's outer defenses, inside the building almost nothing seemed secure. "You could tell a janitor you need a book he had?"

"You wouldn't need the janitor. Everyone with an office here knows where the master key's kept. Getting into the safe, if that's where he keeps it, would be a little harder."

"You don't know the dean's combination?"

"No," Sam said. "The custom is to keep it secret. But I'll get it for you when he calls."

"We'll finish searching the other offices this morning. I think I'll keep his under guard until we can get into his safe."

Nick was due to see Emory Stokes at noon. "You've spent the morning with my colleagues?" Stokes asked. "Nasty little buggers, aren't they? And they're jealous, you know." He gestured to his walls, crowded with pictures of a dated and somewhat tarnished establishment. "They're jealous of people who've lived in the real world."

"Their lives appear more cloistered than yours."

"Well, you see how the land lies, Lieutenant." He paused and began again with an engaging cheekiness. "You'll think I'm a skunk before you're finished, I'm afraid. But a man's got to protect himself. Truth is, my scholarly credentials are not all they might be. Let them start talking 'emeritus' around me," he said defiantly, spinning the dial left, then right, then left again, "and I'll make them talk turkey."

Stokes's safe was stuffed with yellowed newspaper clippings, recounting not his triumphs in the real world but his colleagues' misadventures. "All of this is in the public domain or a matter of public record," he said. "I haven't stolen anything." He pressed Nick to examine his extensive archive. It included many obituaries, of which Norman Clawsen's brother Herschel's appeared to be the most recent.

"This one's particularly choice," Stokes chuckled, handing Nick a folder containing certified copies of two documents and a clipping he had taken care to laminate. The obituary reported the death of Henry Carroll Cumberland, president of the Cumberland County Bank in Carroll, Kentucky. A vigorous man of fifty-two, it said, and from boyhood a strong swimmer, the former mayor of Carroll had been fishing alone when his boat overturned. An autopsy indicated no foul play and established the cause of death as drowning. A marriage license, taken out two weeks after the accident by Bertram Macauley Harding, bachelor, and Beatrice Elizabeth Porter Cumberland, widow, suggested a lack of proper feeling on Mrs. Cumberland's part. A birth certificate issued in Massachusetts for Bertram Macauley Harding, Jr. suggested worse. "The jewel of my collection," Stokes said.

Nick found his cooperation almost overwhelming, and he was grateful when he was able to move on to Bert Harding's office. Bert was dickering for a prime-time current events show with a book-club tie-in; correspondence with potential guests filled every drawer of his desk. "Look at that in-basket," he exulted. "I won't get out of here today. Well, Nick," he said more seriously. "You've come to check out the artillery, right?"

"Right." The dialogue on Bert's show would be terse and virile.

"I keep the only key on my person." Bert walked over to a lacquered tea chest. "And I was in Indonesia when Jake was shot."

"I know. And there's no sign the lock was picked or the doors forced." Nick satisfied himself that this was the case. "Does it look all right to you?"

"Sure does."

"Then open it up."

The brass key clinked against a golden one from Phi Beta Kappa as Bert shook out his watch chain. The inlaid doors of the chest opened to display a curious collection: all the guns were noteworthy, intricately or sleekly beautiful, but none of them worked. Firing pins had been removed from most; others had their barrels filled with solder. Two of them, handsome old automatics, might once have fired the bullet that killed Larson.

"Who does your gunsmithing?" Nick asked.

"Forestiere brothers. You know them?"

Nick did know them. They were the best in New England, a pair of French Canadian identical twins: expert repairs and renovations, collection maintenance (that meant they could get ammunition and parts for anything from a crossbow to a bazooka), *total confidentiality assured.* Their business had fallen off for a while after they added the last line to their box in the yellow pages. Some of their customers thought they wouldn't make a point of it unless there'd been some lapses, but the Forestieres assuaged those doubts and their workshop was always busy.

"Did they fix this Browning?" Nick asked. Of the two possible murder weapons, it was the less neatly altered. Nothing had been done to its works, and no very skilled hand had dribbled solder down its barrel. Any amateur could have fired the gun and sealed it minutes later.

"Yes, some imbecile kid from a local trade school. The Forestieres were trying to apprentice him, but in the end they sent him back for auto mechanics."

Nick returned the gun to the cabinet; the Browning took 9-mm bullets like the one removed from Jake Larson's chest. The other automatic, a Smith and Wesson, was a smaller bore.

"I'll show you the safe next," Bert said, as he locked the gun cabinet. "And then I'll buy you lunch. If that's not a conflict of interest."

"Another time," Nick said. "I'm way behind schedule today."

Harding's safe contained a chamois bag full of uncut diamonds, a box of Krugerrands, a black notebook like the one in Sam's safe with papers for the West Bank conference, including, as Sam's did not, critical notes from an influential Egyptian editor, and an old blue examination book with an *A* on the cover. He held the book thoughtfully. "First exam I took at Marvell. I was scared as hell." Beneath the grade Nick read: "Fine analysis. I'd like to hear more. See me. Tuttle."

TWENTY

ARGARET TORE UP THE LETTER she was writing and debated with herself whether to try again or at all. She knew what she wanted to say to Jake's daughter; she was having some trouble, though, as they said at Marvell, presenting herself. "I was your father's friend . . ."; "I got to know your father well, in the short time he spent here . . ."; "Your father was a fine man. Even people who knew him only briefly, as I did, grieve . . ." Would anyone care to get a letter like that, stilted and dishonest? Yet, honesty was impossible, intrusive, presumptuous, self-dramatizing. Margaret had no desire to tell all, even assuming, she reflected bitterly, she knew what "all" had been. She wanted Karin to have, from a woman of her father's generation, a sense of his life and work, an understanding of him that her mother would not and probably could not provide. Karin deserved that and so did Jake.

She was beginning another draft when her doorbell rang. Exasperated, she buzzed the outer door open without bothering to call down and identify the visitor. Nick Hannibal had cautioned her against doing that: most likely the killer, assuming Jake to be alone, had fired from the hall into his suite, and immediately fled. It was possible, however, he'd seen her with Larson the night before, at the airport or at the Center, and suspected she knew more than she did—but the intercom in her building was perennially out of order and she'd gotten out of the habit of using it. She slipped the wastebasket full of torn and crumpled paper under a table and answered the door.

"Maggie, it must have been awful tough." Bert Harding burst over the threshold and all but embraced her. He seized her shoulders, one in each hand, and held her at arm's length as he volubly condoled her. "You were such great pals. When Al Worth told me you found the body, I mean, you found Jake, it bowled me over. I wish it had been anybody but you, but I betcha none of the others would have handled it so well. Al looks like he's going to pass out whenever he talks about it."

"I thought you were in Indonesia."

"I was, just a little quickie consulting. I got back in time to help Nick Hannibal poke around at the Center this morning, and when I heard you'd found him, I thought I'd come by and tell you"—his eyes closed with emotion and then opened to stare into hers—"that I had some idea what Jake meant to you . . ."

That was right neighborly, Margaret wanted to say, but she suppressed the impulse. "You're very kind."

"I want to tell you that nobody else understands how close you two had become." Was he telling her he'd seen her the morning Jake was killed? Was she so deranged herself that she saw menace in conventional expressions of sympathy?

"Would you like a cup of tea?" She stepped back, freeing herself from his grasp. Would it be possible for her to fling scalding water at another person? If things got to that pass, would hot water stop him? "Or perhaps you'd like coffee? Let me hang up your coat."

"Either one. Whichever you drink." He followed her into the kitchen. "I didn't want you to think nobody at Marvell notices or cares what happens to other people."

"I don't think that."

"I bet nobody else has even called."

Sam Sternberg had called; Lou Stillman also had, to ask whether she was up to going out for dinner that night or if she'd prefer Chinese food at home.

"A few have," she replied evasively.

The doorbell rang before Bert could resume his inquiry or markedly drop it. This time Margaret remembered Nick's advice and disregarded it. Any other person would be most welcome.

"Molly!"

"Sorry I didn't call first. I thought I'd find you at home." Her greeting was much constrained by Harding's presence. "Hello, Bert."

"Why, Molly honey, I didn't know you were in town. I thought you were off in Italy."

"I got homesick, Bert. And the libraries were closing for Carnival and Ash Wednesday, so I took a vacation."

"Well, I expect you girls have a lot to talk about," Bert said, taking his coat from the front closet. "I am most deeply sorry, Maggie, for all you've been through. Bitsy will be calling you soon. You let us know what we can do for you."

"What on earth are you doing here?" Margaret leaned against the door she had closed behind Harding. "What did Nick tell you?"

"He said you'd seen someone you love die under tragic circumstances. You'd do the same for me."

"Molly, I think Bert knows I was there." Margaret needed to account for Harding's visit, and she could not begin to talk about Jake's death.

"Margaret, everyone knows you were there. You *found* him."

"I mean he knows I was there before . . ."

"You think he's the killer?" Molly had been alarmed to find Bert in Margaret's apartment but she'd dismissed her fears.

Bert was impetuous and effusive, a type once called ple-
thoric, more likely than another to act on a kind impulse.
She'd almost convinced herself.

"Maybe."

Molly tried to be reasonable. "He may have been the only
one at the Center who guessed how close you were. He's an
amorous type himself, attuned to that side of life. It's part of
being political."

"I disagree. I'm political and I hadn't noticed it myself until
it happened."

"You notice other people." Molly remembered how tact-
lessly encouraging her friend had been at the most trying
moments last summer.

"Oh, the two of you," Margaret said. "I should have tucked
you into bed myself, you were making each other so miserable."

Molly marveled at this toughness, this lack of self-pity. "Do
you want to talk about Jake?"

"No. Yes. He was good and kind and fair and smart. He
was married, can you imagine, to a woman who left him for
an orthodontist. I guess he would have been faithful to her if
she hadn't, even though she reminded him of Samuel
Gompers."

This was not a nonsequitur to Molly, who agreed it was
very sad. It was a strangely inadequate bereavement and she
could think of no better comfort than to acknowledge its
strangeness. "I came home," she said, "because I love and
admire you. I'm glad I was in a position to know what had
happened. You won't be comforted as people usually are."

"That's right, no wake, no open casket, no crowd of
ghouls."

"Wakes may be tasteless," Molly said, "but they pass the
time. They force you to see people. They force you back into
the community that will ultimately heal you."

"We weren't a couple. We weren't even living in sin. Do

you know that the teachers' contract covers that now? 'Member of the household' counts as immediate family for the purposes of bereavement leave."

"In Newnham?" Molly was surprised. "But I suppose the language covers more traditional extended families as well."

"Of course. How in hell do you think it passed? But we didn't have a past. That's almost worse than not having a future."

"Yes, I can imagine."

"I almost envy those widows. You know the ones I mean. They haven't spoken to their husbands for years before they died except to ask them to change the channel. They haven't slept with them since their last child was conceived forty years ago, but they'd fallen in love once and got married and they must have some memories. I can't remember a thing."

"SHE HASN'T CRIED AT ALL. She seems anesthetized." Molly and Nick were walking along the river in a pearly twilight. From the riverbank came the wet earthy smell of quickening mud. Molly had left Margaret to dine alone with Lou Stillman and planned to stop back later in the evening. If Margaret wanted company, she'd stay overnight. "Losing a memory's like losing at least part of your mind, and Margaret's very worried about it. I've been thinking about virginity and amnesia."

"Was this her first experience of sex?" Nick asked.

"I think it may have been. Didn't Hera regain her virginity each year by bathing in a sacred spring?" Molly taught the Renaissance and Reformation and relied on Nick for knowledge of the classics.

"Yes, the spring Kanathos."

"Did the waters just restore her physically or did they wash away her memory too and leave her inexperienced?"

"An interesting question my Jesuit teachers omitted to discuss. I suspect there were things Zeus preferred she'd forget."

"I think Margaret's blocking an unhappy experience. I suspect that, at her age, consummation might be difficult."

Nick pondered that. "You think she's denying something she regards as a failure?"

"That's more like her, surely," Molly reasoned, "than neurotic guilt about sex. She's not a captive of her background in any other way. I almost hope, if things were very awkward, that she doesn't remember."

"No, it would be better if she could remember, and accept whatever they did as expressions of love." They walked in silence after that, wondering what comfort they could possibly give her.

"I would like to nail the killer," Nick said finally. "It's a smarmy crowd at the Center."

"Catch me up," Molly said, having not the least idea herself what to do about the psychological problem.

"The killings may not be connected. Larson and Llewellyn don't seem to have had a great deal in common, and neither murder may involve the Center, nevertheless . . ." He led her off the path closer to the water.

"Nevertheless, the more you see of Marvell, the more irresistible the suspicion . . ." She picked up a flat stone and gave it to him to skip.

"Thank you. Wouldn't you like to try it yourself?"

"No. I'll watch. Oh, three skips, very nice. Now, about the irresistible Center?"

"The Center's got state-of-the-art security. Larson's killer must be a person able to enter the building in an ordinary way before it's locked at midnight, stay overnight and go about his business inconspicuously the next day."

"You know what Margaret thinks?" Molly asked, unable for the moment to separate her perspective from her friend's.

"Yes, she wants a federal indictment of the Teamsters. Murder has been prosecuted as a violation of the victim's civil rights before, but rarely in a labor dispute."

"She needs to derive some public good from Jake's death. The private aftermath is so ghastly. And, Nick, if Tom Franchetti, who is a truck driver, had already murdered Dick Llewellyn *qua* jealous husband and was working up to plead insanity, couldn't he have been induced to kill again for his union?"

"The Teamsters wouldn't employ a psychotic kid as a hit man. But Larson himself spent a certain amount of time with Donna, some of it at Harding's insistence. And Harding, I found out from some remarkable backbiting at Marvell, might have had motives to kill both men."

"Really?" Maybe Bert was more than impulsive.

"Llewellyn, we know from his humorous book review, had followed Harding's sallies into Latin America from the beginning. And he was getting interested in a topic Harding once explored for the Chileans—rural protest adapted to an urban setting."

"There's a lot of comparative work on that, some of it done with very dubious funding for even more dubious purposes."

"The Chileans probably paid better than the average grant," Nick said. "Margaret also mentioned, in connection with something else, that Jake spoke Spanish." Nick spun this out confidently. "His passport shows that he'd spent time in Peru where Dick Llewellyn had been with the Peace Corps, and in Costa Rica and Honduras. In all three places American trade unionists are helping build 'democratic infrastructure' and who knows what else."

"Harding's been involved with very nasty governments in that part of the world."

"I'll tell you what piqued my interest. I saw an old blue book in Harding's safe. In among some pricey and easily negotiable souvenirs, I found an exam he'd written years ago for

Caleb Tuttle, with an invitation to come and talk about the Cold War underneath the *A.*"

"Harding has a brain."

"Tuttle evidently thought so. Sam said he's the last of the heroic generation."

"He is the last. Imagine Alvin Worth making a cost-benefit analysis of fascism or Clawsen being parachuted into Rumania. During the Second World War, the best people at Marvell went into the OSS."

"And continued with the CIA? Recruiting their most promising students?"

"Not Tuttle," Molly said emphatically. "He's always held that scholarship and intelligence gathering are incompatible activities. He's never worked on a project he couldn't publish without taking a formal leave of absence."

"Maybe he wanted to warn Harding that others would try to recruit him."

"Warning him, yes, that's more consistent with Tuttle's character. I wonder who the talent scout was?"

"How about Emory Stokes?"

"Emory Stokes." The idea stopped her in her tracks. "Nick, if I thought Emory Stokes had the least responsibility for American security, I'd be terrified. I'd volunteer myself rather than leave it to him."

"Stokes has something on Harding. His wife's first husband, a wealthy older man, drowned when she was more than three months pregnant with Bertram junior."

"Children, especially young children, are often adopted by their stepfathers."

"That's a charitable thought," he said. "But, I admired pictures of Harding's children today, closely. He has to be the boy's natural father. The coroner who did the autopsy after the first husband's death was vigilant enough or dubious enough to make sure there was water in his lungs."

"Or crooked enough to say there was?" They had reached

the footbridge where they'd met Margaret and Jake on a desolate night soon after Dick Llewellyn's death. Crossing the bridge, they stopped and looked down at the river, pink and violet like the cloudless evening sky it reflected. "Was the coroner crooked?" Molly repeated. The beauty around them was not comforting; it left them somber and subdued.

"I suppose he might have been. And you see, all this happened and may still be spoken of in Cumberland County, Kentucky, close to the GM plant Larson had been visiting almost weekly."

"And in a border state where Llewellyn often worked," she reminded him.

"Harding was in the BPL on the afternoon of Llewellyn's murder," Nick said, releasing her hand and tapping his fist on the railing of the bridge. "I'm certain of that, but—" he continued more tentatively—"but he was in Jakarta when Larson was killed. He did visit Franchetti at Bridgewater though, through the complaisance of his friend the warden. The public defender found out and put a stop to it, but not until Bert had several sessions with Tommy."

"Franchetti has an alibi, but not a great one, for the first murder, for which he also has a compelling motive," Molly suggested. "Nick, suppose Harding, during his visits to Bridgewater, dropped hints, primed Franchetti to kill Larson while he himself was very publicly abroad—hoping to pin Llewellyn's murder on him too?"

ALVIN WORTH AND NORMAN CLAWSEN were approaching the same conclusion. "I think Bert's responsible, as responsible as if he pulled the trigger himself," Worth said indignantly.

"Maybe he did pull the trigger himself."

"He was in Jakarta," Worth reminded his friend regretfully.

"Says who? Some corrupt Indonesian who'd sell his women for an invitation to the Center? I'm by no means certain Bert's always where he claims to be."

"He came back a full week before his secretary expected him, I know that much. She'd been told to relay his calls to Bangkok this week."

"Bangkok? I never heard he'd be nosing around Bangkok. Emory thought he was coming back through Islamabad. Alvin, have you any idea of the whereabouts of that very gifted young Thai?" Clawsen had trouble remembering Tikibinitantari's full name and he hesitated to call so remarkable a talent simply Tiki.

"He's having a rest. He's determined to move from microanalysis to macroanalysis. Having worked so brilliantly on methodology, and having completed a micro-level dissertation ahead of schedule, his mentors thought he needed a rest before tackling a macro-level problem."

"Alvin, *where* is he?"

"He's in seclusion in the Berkshires."

"In a funny farm?"

"On a farm recently purchased by his family and staffed with responsible people. Complete rest has been prescribed, Norman. They won't let him have pens or pencils, and the boy bisected a Laffer curve with a Pareto optimum using two colors of toothpaste."

"Fantastic."

"It's a real contribution. They called me and I made sure they photographed everything before they washed down the wall. But think, Norman, he'll be able to teach methods, micro and macro. And now that that little tart from Oral Roberts has taken the Hoover Institute job, he'll be irresistible."

"A triple threat," Clawsen murmured.

"What are you implying? That he's killed twice already?"

"By no means, Al. Nothing of the sort. I'm hoping the glory he brings to Marvell will partially offset the scandal of Harding's arrest."

TWENTY-ONE

"I'M BEING SET UP, HANNIBAL." Bert Harding stormed into Nick's office carrying a large brown envelope and a copy of his best-selling attack on civilian review boards. The flattering likeness of the author on the dust jacket of that minor classic had gotten him past the sergeant at the desk and up the elevator to the Homicide Unit. "Somebody's trying to pin this murder on me."

"Only one of them?" Nick asked, rising to meet him and firmly closing the door Harding had flung open.

"Damned if I know, maybe both. But I don't see the point of this." He handed Nick the envelope, mailed the previous week, library rate, from Detroit. "Listen, Nick, I can prove I was watching Balinese dancers with half of the Indonesian Ministry of Defense when Larson was shot."

"I'm sure you can. Sit down, Bert. Make yourself comfortable while I have a look at this."

"My secretary and I are the only people at the Center who've handled the contents, so far as I know."

"Fine." Nick opened the envelope and took out a quantity of xeroxed paper. The cover letter read:

Dear Professor Harding:
   I was so surprised when you called last week that I forgot to tell you how much I enjoy you whenever I see you on televi-

sion. One often hears that nationally-known professors neglect their teaching responsibilities. You must be the exception
that proves the rule.

Mr. Larson, as I told you last week, had already been here
when you called, and, even without your kind intercession, he
had been given every assistance by me and my staff in locating
the documents he needed to complete his project for your
course. After he left, one of the archivists found some other
papers she thought relevant to his topic, and because we did
not have a Boston address for him, I have taken the liberty of
sending them to you.

I hope it will not be burdensome for you to convey them to
him, but considering the lengths to which you are willing to go
to help your students, I felt sure I could impose upon you.

The letter was signed, "Yours sincerely and with the great-
est admiration, Mary Beth Tomlinson, Archivist-in-Chief,
Public Records Room, Detroit Public Library."

"I was in Jakarta the day that call was made."

"It's possible to call Detroit from Jakarta."

"Well, I didn't and whoever did used the phone in my
office. I checked with the phone company."

"Do you have any idea what's going on?"

"None, that's why I'm asking you. You've got a nice view
up here." Harding gazed resolutely down on Berkeley Street
while Nick read through the papers.

"I assume Larson was not doing research for you on any
subject remotely connected with obstacles to farmer-labor
alliances," he asked, handing them back to Harding.

"Hell, no. I'm not doing much teaching this spring, only
one seminar, and he's not in it."

"I'll be frank with you, Bert."

"You going to read me my rights first?"

"If you like, but I don't think it'll come to that. I've been
surprised by the lack of collegiality I've found at the Center. I
expected your colleagues would cooperate with the police,
naturally, but I also expected some solidarity. People should

be wracking their brains to figure out how an intruder could have killed Larson. Instead, they're all maligning each other."

"I'm not maligning anybody."

"Here again, you're the exception. Look, Bert, both Llewellyn and Larson had worked in Latin America. Larson advised several agricultural unions there, in connection with some UAW project on grass-roots democracy. Were any labor organizers killed during your time in Chile?"

"They play hardball in Chile. People get killed all the time."

"I wasn't asking about local customs."

"I didn't finger anybody, if that's what you mean." Bert looked almost sheepish. "All I did was create a profile."

"A profile?"

"Yeah, you know, a Platonic form, an ideal-type of the optimally effective agitator. I expect they arrested some people who fit the description. What else would they have wanted it for?"

Nick said nothing. Harding's work seemed the worst sort of hit-and-run meddling. It was one thing to back a government and fight for it. Something else to practice counterinsurgency hypothetically on an expense account.

"I know what you're thinking." Bert was angry now, not apologetic. "You're thinking, 'The brave man kills it with a sword, the coward with a word . . .' You're lucky, Hannibal. Words are all I've got. I didn't kill either of those guys." His big body seemed diminished as he turned to leave.

"I don't think you did. Wait, Bert, before you go." It was easier to talk with Harding deflated. "Suppose Larson really did have trouble getting the records he needed. Someone who was trying to help him could have used your name. You are well-known."

"Could be. Emory Stokes makes dinner reservations in my name every time he goes to Washington. Then he tells the maître d' I said to start without me." Harding chuckled, pleased with himself again. He'd known about Stokes's ploy for years and never resented it: he liked to think that people relied on his prestige. "You could be right, Nick. Maybe that's all it was."

"I'll look into this for you and keep you posted." Nick walked out to the elevators with Harding and watched the numbers over the door flash in descending order until Harding reached the ground floor. Then, he went back to his office and called the obliging archivist in Detroit.

She said, as he thought she might, that she hadn't recognized Professor Harding's voice at first. The timbre seemed rather different over the phone. If it hadn't been for that drawl he'd never lost, she'd have never known it was *the* Bertram Harding. She was horrified to learn of Larson's death and promised to send copies of all the documents he had consulted. The name Richard Llewellyn meant nothing to her.

"How's MARGARET?" Nick telephoned Molly partly out of concern for Margaret and partly in the hope that she'd be free to spend the night with him.

"She's bearing up. She gave three elementary school principals protracted hell this morning about the charmlessness of their window decorations. I think it's a good sign."

"An excellent sign. Do you think you need to stay with her tonight?"

"Actually, I'd be in the way. Her dreary sister Nora is in town to see her doctors and she'll be staying here."

"That's even better news. Can you meet me at the Center in an hour or so? Caleb Tuttle called in from Prague. He does have a gun in his safe and he told Sam the combination, which, Sam says, anyone who knew Tuttle could have guessed."

"It's a date?"

"Yes. Eight, five, forty-five."

"August? No, the eighth of May, European style, 1945. Of course."

"That's right. V-E Day, what else would a war hero pick? I'll have the gun examined, and I want to look through Larson's rooms, too. Somebody impersonated Bert Harding to find out what documents Larson used the last time he was in Detroit."

"Margaret has one of his notebooks here. It's full of caricatures, including some hilarious sketches of Bert."

"Tell her I'd like to see that too, would you? I think Larson rarely missed the point."

"I'M GLAD YOU'RE HERE." Sam Sternberg was waiting for Nick outside the dean's office. "Bert Harding told me his name was used to impress a librarian. It seems that somebody used mine to rent a car."

"Did you lose a credit card and forget to report it?"

"No, the Center has an account with Avis. If you know the charge number and the code, all you need to do is give them one of the authorized names."

"When did this happen?"

"The car was picked up in Cincinnati on the Thursday before Dick Llewellyn was killed and left that weekend in Boston, at one of the spots where you can park the car yourself and drop the papers and keys in a box. The bill just came in, and Caleb's secretary asked me about it."

"And you've been nowhere near Cincinnati and given out the numbers to no one."

"That's right."

"That is strange. Let's see about the gun."

Caleb Tuttle's Luger, captured in an encounter he thought

of often and spoke of never, lay wrapped in a cloth in a blackened tin box beside other mementos, several medals, a belt buckle embossed *Gott mit uns* and a badge claiming the same sponsorship in Ukrainian, some amber beads, the limestone fossil of a fern still common in Ruthenia and a woman's wedding ring. Oddly, given the convenient proximity of an oiled cloth, it appeared that an attempt had been made to clean the gun with a paper tissue tamped down by a pencil. The eraser had worn through the Kleenex and left deposits of lint and pink rubber on the inside of the barrel. "Dumb," Nick concluded, and ballistics would add little to his analysis.

"JAKE WAS AN EXEMPLARY PAPER WRITER," Molly said. She sat at Larson's desk in his suite at the Center, looking through his labor history notes. "He put together an excellent bibliography, noting which of Marvell's libraries had the book." She went to the wall of bookshelves. "And he checked off the books he'd already taken out. That's odd."

"What?" Nick was going through the looseleaf journal in which Larson kept a record of his trips to Kentucky. He had already found, among the addresses and phone numbers of local journalists, the editor of the *Carroll Weekly Sentinel.* "What's odd?"

"There's a title that's supposed to be in five different libraries at Marvell, two of them noncirculating. It was missing from all of them."

"Maybe it's very good and gets stolen. I suppose that happens even at Marvell."

"Alas, yes, but it can't be that good. It was written by Norman Clawsen. Jake probably thought it would be courteous to have a look at it. What are you finding?"

"He must have known every reporter in Cumberland County, Kentucky. He copied out a longish passage from the

Supreme Court case I told you about, involving competing unions. And he drew Margaret constantly when he was away from her. Here, look at this."

"O-oh," Molly breathed a long, sorrowful syllable. "He saw the essential Margaret." She studied the sketches, then handed the notebook back to Nick. "He must have cared for her to draw her like that."

"The feeling and the talent look very real to me."

"Are they evidence?" she asked. "Can I have them framed for her? Beautifully? Expensively?"

"I'll make sure nothing happens to them. Is Margaret's memory returning?"

"I don't think so," Molly said. "But I called a gynecologist today while she was out driving her hypochondriac sister to her innumerable specialists. I mentioned no names of course, just her age. The doctor said there'd be considerable atrophy. Consummation might take months."

"Months?" That would be a daunting project. "Months, really?"

"Yes. I think I'll ask her to come back to Italy with me. It's a more demonstrative culture. Lots of kissing and touching, more, well, more . . ."

"Polymorphous. It's a good idea."

"I don't know of a particular fresco that will jog her memory," she explained. "It's more the ambience."

"I think it's a very good idea."

"Did Margaret tell you about the man on the roof of the parking garage?" Margaret, unable to talk about Jake, wanted to discuss every detail of the case and Molly had been happy to hear her out. Thinking, she recognized, can distract, even when it's powerless to console.

"Yes, and he wasn't the alleged rapist, because that man has been caught and identified in a lineup by several women. On the other hand, in support of the Teamster theory, a number of people thought her description of the guy on the roof sounded like somebody who's done an amount of professional strongarming among the freight handlers at the airport."

"Really? The police took two hours, after she reported the stalled car, to tell her it was gone. Don't you think that's suspicious?"

"Probably just inefficient. Molly, I'm sure this killing originated here. There are a couple of possible murder weapons right in the building, and ammunition near at hand."

"Not on hand at Marvell?" Molly objected.

"Oh, yes. Not far from here. ROTC's been permitted back on campus, you know, but quietly, without fanfare. Sam tells me the pro-ROTC faction's biding its time, hoping to rededicate the building that was closed after the sit-in in the sixties. In anticipation of that gala, they've collected memorabilia from all the campaigns in which Marvell men distinguished themselves."

"Revolutionary war muskets, cannonballs from Old Ironsides, officers' sidearms?"

"That's right. And ammunition—for all standard issue Allied and enemy automatics."

"You can get bullets for a vintage Luger in the old ROTC building?" Molly said. "Marvell really is the hub!"

"It does present a wealth of opportunities," he agreed. "Molly, you read Llewellyn's manuscript. Is it related, at all, to the research Jake was doing?"

"Only tangentially. Dick Llewellyn worked on agrarian protest and Jake, you saw in the papers Harding showed you, was interested in farmer-labor relations, when they cooperated, when they fought."

"That may be close enough." Hannibal thought he'd let those notions simmer awhile. "Let's pack up Larson's papers and look at the caricatures after dinner."

Later that evening, they saw what Jake had seen in the faces of the Marvell faculty: weariness, anger, detachment, amusement, petulance, stupefaction and, on one countenance, abject terror.

TWENTY-TWO

ARLY THE NEXT AFTERNOON Audrey Clawsen entered her husband's office at the Center for Participatory Politics without knocking. He was straightening the picture over his wall safe and spun round when he heard the door open. "I've asked you not to interrupt me at work."

"What were you putting in your safe?"

"The cleaning lady left the picture crooked. You know I can't stand it when things are out of place." He did not step forward to meet her. "I have a lot to do, Audrey. I won't be home for dinner."

"Norman, who is she?"

"The cleaning lady?"

"The woman you met at the convention last December. You were never in your own hotel room."

"Naturally not. I was seeing people, dialoguing, exchanging ideas and hypotheses. Here, these pictures came today." He thrust a pile of black and white glossies into her hand. "Here I am at lunch with the chairman of the political science department at Yale. Here I am at the concluding banquet Sunday night with the most innovative people from Chapel Hill."

"I don't believe you slept in your own room. I was never able to reach you."

"There were breakfast meetings at seven and evening sessions that went on well past midnight. Knowledge in political science is increasing exponentially."

She was unmoved.

"Very fast," he added.

"I know what an exponent is, Norman. It's like squared or cubed or to the nth degree. And that's how fed up I am with you, to the nth degree. Tell me this. If you don't have a woman in Detroit, why did you rush back there right before that sex kitten turned up at the Hardings'?"

"I didn't go to Detroit. I told you I had to fill in for somebody who got sick at Columbia."

"You flew to Detroit, Norman. The travel agent called about your frequent flier bonus."

"All right, if you must know. I went to a funeral in Detroit."

"I don't believe you. We don't know anyone in Detroit."

"He was an old Jewish guy. Audrey, when my parents lost the farm, our dairy farm, they couldn't afford to keep me in school."

"Yes? You've told me about that."

"We used to sell our milk to a coop that sold it to the chain of supermarkets this old fellow owned. The people who ran the coop told him how gifted I was, how promising, and he lent me the money to complete my education. He practically gave it to me, in an interest-free loan. When I heard he'd died, I thought I ought to attend his funeral."

"I'm your wife, Norman. If he helped you, I should have paid my respects to him too. I should have been at your side. You should have taken me with you."

"You'd have been out of place, Audrey. I felt out of place myself."

"You're lying. But I didn't tell that detective anything."

"Hannibal did question you?"

"Yes." She was standing at the door of his office, wearing a knitted hat and gloves and her loden car coat. "Who is he,

Norman? What does he want with us?" She moved closer to him.

"Hannibal's some hotshot cop Bert Harding's cultivating." He retreated behind his desk. She hated that, that he never stayed close to her or spoke as if he meant his words for her alone. "He apparently thinks someone at the Center murdered those two men."

"Don't worry," she stepped nearer to him. "I told him you were out of town at a convention over the New Year's weekend."

"Good. And you told him I was home with you last Sunday?"

"No. I said that you were working late and that you must have slept on the living room sofa because you're too considerate to disturb me when you get back late at night."

"And why in God's name did you say that?"

"Because I didn't know where the hell you were. What did you want me to say?" She took off her hat and gloves and threw them on his desk. "That we made love all weekend? That you'd left our bed only to get more champagne?" Her voice rose, stopped in a sob and began again in a taunting monotone. "How about, 'I'll never forget the night of March fifth, Lieutenant. It was a night of clinging, panting, thrusting, burning ecstasy. At the first rays of dawn on the morning of the sixth I fell asleep in my husband's arms, spent with rapture'? Should I have said that? Would you like that better?"

"Audrey, where do you find the trash you read?"

"Don't condescend to me, you bastard. Emory says you're not having an affair, but I don't believe him either."

"You told a detective from Homicide you weren't sure when I got home on the night a murder was committed in the building where I work?" Clawsen sank aghast into the chair behind his desk. "As it happens, I was out helping Alvin look for Tikibooboo, who'd escaped from his handlers, but

Alvin won't say that because he doesn't want to implicate the Great Yellow Hope. He'll throw me to the wolves rather than risk losing him."

"I don't care. I want to see what's in your safe."

"All right. Fine. I'll open it for you."

Clawsen sat at his desk with his head in his hands as his wife perused his sex manuals. She was not a stupid woman, and she correctly inferred, after comparing the marginal notes with her own recollections, that Norman had been faithful to her.

"You're not in love," she announced, replacing the books in the safe.

"I am not in love," he assured her.

"There's no other woman."

"No woman means more to me than you do."

"Oh, Norman," she said. "I was so afraid of losing you."

"There's no one else." This was a fact he hoped he need not repeat again.

"I believe you, dear. Please, please, Norman, try to get home a little earlier tonight."

"I'm dining out tonight, I'm afraid. I've been asked to address the political science majors at Scattergood College on the statistical probability of a woman president in their lifetime."

MOLLY WAS SPENDING the day at Scattergood. She took the opportunity, since she was in Massachusetts during term time, to meet with the students she'd be advising when she returned. It was simpler, too, to talk with her chairman about next year's courses than to correspond about them, and she had promised to brief Scattergood's new president, the physicist Clara Meicklejohn, on the festivities planned in Italy for the centenary of Enrico Fermi's birth.

Nick was in Boston, pulling together several bits of information; he sensed that a solution was taking shape. The package promised by the Detroit archivist arrived before noon. Larson had been looking into a conflict between strikers and rural strikebreakers. These appeared to be searching interviews with men on both sides of a major brawl. He'd show them to Molly tonight.

He'd not looked, for some weeks, at Richard Llewellyn's papers. He turned now to the notebook Llewellyn brought with him to the Boston Public Library the day he was murdered and found in it the titles of some journal articles and a list of municipal libraries: Cleveland, Detroit, Pittsburgh, Buffalo, Gary. That fit. Llewellyn was moving away from purely agrarian themes. Margaret had mentioned it. Harding had not been surprised to hear it. Most likely all the members of the search committee knew.

At four, Avis confirmed that the car rented in Sam Sternberg's name had been returned, not to their main branch at the airport, but to a smaller lot near the Greyhound Bus Terminal.

And then Molly called. "Nick, the book that Larson couldn't find at Marvell . . . It's Norman Clawsen's first book. He's lecturing here this afternoon and his collected works are on display in the library."

"He's inordinately vain about his scholarship. If it isn't up to snuff, he probably stole the Marvell copies himself."

"I've only glanced at it, but it looks terrific. Whoever conducted these interviews was clairvoyant. It can't be his own work."

"That would give him an even better reason to seize every copy he could get his hands on."

"A compelling reason."

"Molly, where are you?"

"At a pay phone in the library."

"Are you alone?"

"Yes."

"Has anyone seen you with the book?"

"No." She had never heard him speak so peremptorily.

"Are you sure?" Fear made his voice harsh.

"Yes, dear, quite sure."

"All right then. Misshelve it. Put it where no one would expect to find it and go directly to the most crowded place on campus. What would that be?"

"The student center, probably."

"Wait for me there."

On most days it took Molly more than an hour to drive out to Scattergood College, but she was not surprised to see Nick, forty minutes later, saunter into the student center and ask her if she'd like an early dinner. "I'd love it," she said. "Let me make sure the library has the books I need to put on reserve when I get back and then I don't have to do another thing here until the fall."

She took him into the stacks to Scattergood's extensive collection of first editions by American women scholars and withdrew a teal blue volume, wedged between works by Ruth Benedict and Margaret Mead. "Good spot," Nick said, folding it into the newspaper he was carrying.

They went to the library's front desk, and Molly introduced Nick to the librarian, who was as impressed as she expected her to be. Scattergood might be a fiercely feminist institution, Molly reflected, but nothing conferred status there more reliably than an attentive hunk. The librarian wistfully wished them a pleasant evening and forgot to check their belongings.

"CLAWSEN'S BOOK IS NOTHING but a rearrangement of these interviews," Molly said, "with an introduction that says they speak powerfully for themselves." They had returned to

Nick's office and he was showing her the papers Jake had been working on in Detroit. "WPA oral histories are often good, but these are exceptionally sensitive. I wonder what happened to the person who did them."

"A woman struggling to get her family through the Depression who never had another chance to do research," Nick suggested.

"Or a man who didn't survive the war. It's sad."

"This explains Llewellyn's death too, doesn't it?"

"He used sources much like these, citing them, of course, and acknowledging his debts to them in quite a touching way."

"I have his manuscript here." Nick flipped to the end. "He knew Clawsen's book. It's in his bibliography. And his next project, both Margaret and Clawsen told me early on, was to investigate confrontations like these between the rural and the urban poor."

"Clawsen brought that up spontaneously?" Molly was surprised to hear that. Clawsen did not strike her as a soul yearning for chastisement.

"He couldn't resist, because it strengthened the case against Bert Harding. He's been advising the Chileans, remember, on ways to keep their peasants leery of outside agitators."

"Harding is beneath contempt. No wonder he cancels courses on mass murder. But if Llewellyn was turning to such a topic and he'd already found WPA sources useful, he'd get to these interviews sooner or later."

"Sooner," Nick said. "He planned to go to Detroit this spring."

"Isn't that where Clawsen says he was in December?"

"Yes. At a four-day convention. The only hard evidence of his presence puts him at the opening lunch and the concluding dinner. That leaves him seventy, maybe eighty, hours to get back and forth. Somebody who knew the Center's Avis account number used Sam Sternberg's name to take a car from Cincinnati, a few hundred miles south of Detroit, to Boston that weekend."

"Clawsen looks as if his name could be Sternberg," Molly observed. "It's certainly credible."

"Yes, it is. And his wife made up a sad little story about the night Jake was shot. She's not the sort of woman who could tell a policeman an outright lie, so she said her husband was too considerate to come to bed after working late."

"I wouldn't want a husband that considerate."

"Never fear," he promised. "But I should call the bus company before we go home." Greyhound offered three departures daily from Boston to Detroit. The trip took twenty hours and cost $103.

"Llewellyn was killed before four on Saturday afternoon," Molly said. "He'd have easily made it back by Sunday night. But could he have flown to Detroit with a weapon like that in his luggage?"

"He didn't need to take the dagger to Detroit. He may have kept it in the same locker before and after the murder. The Greyhound terminal's a five-minute walk from the library."

"It was clever to separate the dagger from the stones. It made it look more and more like Harding, framing Franchetti in a pointed but unconvincing way and taking no chances with the jewels. Is any ammunition, in fact, missing from the ROTC building?"

"I'll check that first thing tomorrow morning."

TWENTY-THREE

WHEN NORMAN CLAWSEN ARRIVED at the Center the next morning, he asked the dean's secretary to let him into Mr. Tuttle's office; he recollected that Caleb had a book he needed to consult. "Certainly," she said, handing him a bunch of keys she kept in her top desk drawer. "You're bright and early this morning. It must be hard for professors to work with all these disruptions. We've had the police here constantly."

"They were very thorough the other day, I heard," he said as he took the keys from her.

"Goodness, yes. But they left the room tidy, thank heaven."

"When will he be back?" Tuttle had been kind to him in his first years at Marvell, encouraged him, sought him out, spoken to him from time to time of his experiences in the war. He had grown cooler over the years, as if Clawsen had somehow disappointed him.

"He'll be back in May."

Clawsen let himself into Tuttle's office and walked twice around the book-lined walls, stopping finally in the center of a worn rug. Caleb Tuttle had told him long ago that Balkan designs were more representational than those found in Turkish or Persian weaving: strange purple birds and rust-colored hares hid among gray ferns on the border of his carpet. This was not the room in which he had first met the great man—money had been raised to build the Center some years after Clawsen came to Marvell—but it was as like the old room as a new one could be made. Caleb Tuttle, the famous liberal, hated change.

Clawsen remembered their first interview: Tuttle had written, praising his book and asking that he come and talk with him about teaching at Marvell. That had been before search committees, Clawsen recalled, wondering how he'd fare in today's job market with today's procedures. Tuttle had asked him about himself, about his family, and toward the end of the interview, when Norman admired the rug, he had said, "It's good of its kind. It doesn't pretend to be something it's not."

He had thought then of telling him the truth, about his real family, about his plagiarized dissertation, about the work he wanted to do and feared to undertake, but he had quickly and irrevocably decided against telling the truth. He looked for a last time around the Dean's office and closed the door softly behind him.

"I'll be glad when he's back," the secretary said, taking the keys from Clawsen. "I miss him."

"We all miss him." He walked down the long corridor, past Emory's office, past Harding's, then down several flights of stairs to his own. Through his sole window, he saw Hannibal drive into a visitor's space in the parking lot.

The poplars that surrounded the lot were coming into leaf, but he could follow the detective's movements. He was not heading for the Center; instead he took the path that led through an alley of lilac bushes to the old ROTC building. The bushes, still dormant, would be covered with purple blossoms in May when Caleb Tuttle returned, deep purple, like the herons on his rug. The Ukraine was marshy, Tuttle had said, with many long-legged birds: heavy tanks sank up to their turrets in the marshes and waterfowl perched on them, unconcernedly. Clawsen sat on the edge of his walnut desk and waited.

He had been waiting, it seemed, since Herschel's funeral. His brother Sol had called him—Sol had been the wild one. When he began studying for the rabbinate, everybody said they'd have expected it of Nahum, the quieter, more studious boy, but never of Sollie, and Sol's manner was not pastoral even now. He'd announced the death and the time and place of the service, Friday morning in a big downtown synagogue, and told him he ought to be there. Clawsen said he would not come, and the brothers hung up simultaneously. He couldn't miss the Hardings' houseparty. He'd been sure Bert had something up his sleeve: he'd anticipated, if not Susannah Mae herself, something equally egregious.

Still, he'd known he had to go to Detroit. He'd liked Herschel more than he liked the others; he disliked Sol and hated his sisters. He'd come and go and try to be back for Bert's party. He'd go but avoid the family altogether, and that's what he'd done. That's what he'd been doing, killing time before the service began, when he saw Jake Larson going into the main city library, the library where he'd researched his own dissertation.

He'd overheard Larson and Margaret Donahue talking in the Center's cafeteria the previous week about the strike he'd studied, but their conversation hadn't really rattled him. A hotshot graduate student like Llewellyn might check into all the sources, but what records would a guy like Larson consult? Even when he saw Larson enter the library that morning, he hadn't altogether lost heart. No one could say he'd acted hastily. He'd made careful inquiries; he'd made sure Larson had actually consulted the interviews he'd passed off as his own. Even now it seemed incredible to him. Who'd ever imagine a midcareer fellow would take the trouble to dig up sources like that? Usually they just read back issues of *The*

Economist. Clawsen sat, motionless, on his desk, staring out the window as his colleagues began to arrive.

"PROFESSOR CLAWSEN CAME IN early this morning," Tuttle's pleasant, capable secretary told Nick Hannibal. "But he called a few minutes ago to say he wasn't feeling well. He said he might be going home. Shall I ring his office and ask him to wait for you?"

"Don't trouble," Nick said. "I know where his office is. If I miss him there, I'll catch up with him later."

"It's no trouble," she said, lifting the receiver.

"Don't disturb him." Nick depressed the phone's cradle gently, interrupting the call.

"As you wish."

Hannibal did not start to run until he was out of the Center; he caught sight of Clawsen a few blocks ahead of him, fleeing into the subway station, but he reached the platform too late to see which train he had taken. Clawsen could go to the airport or to any of several commuter rail stations; more shrewdly, he could change lines repeatedly and lose himself underground. Nick returned to the Center and called in an all-points bulletin from his car. Then he drove north toward the suburban terminus. Clawsen had said he was going home.

NORMAN CLAWSEN WAS HURRYING HOME. He gave his body over to the lurching rhythm of the subway car: he knew he could not hasten its progress, but its motion comforted him. He leaned against the door, directly under the stenciled notice that instructed him not to lean against the door, and fell through its sliding panels as soon as they opened. He scrambled to his feet and dashed along the train platform toward the escalator. If only he could get there before the detective.

The bronze wild creatures set into the station floor no longer resembled his colleagues: they were simply animals, animals who chirped, croaked and hissed their welcome, and he was glad to be back among them. He made his way more composedly now toward the pasture. Almost home . . .

But Hannibal was there, too. This time the detective did not park his car carefully within the white lines. He drove right up to an exit and burst through the door. Clawsen reached the escalator that led to the platform with the *trompe l'oeil* mural. He saw Hannibal racing up a ramp that curved around the escalators and ended also at the painted wall. Squadrons of police cars surrounded the building, and Clawsen thought he saw policemen surging through every door. The glass elevator cages hung suspended, so full, it seemed to him, of blue-coated bodies that they could not move.

Then, at the top of the escalator he saw the dairy herd, just beyond the glass and aluminum doors, a wall of doors like those that led to the buses. Behind them, cows were grazing in a field dappled with sun and shadow, dotted with pink and purple clover. Other flowers grew in the pasture too, but their names escaped him and Audrey had to remind him, though, of course, he knew them all from his boyhood on the farm. Hawkweed and beetleweed. Adder's tongue, coltsfoot and Jacob's ladder. Pearly everlasting and flower-of-an-hour. Queen-of-the-prairie.

The detective Bert Harding said was so sharp was calling his name. The cows were lowing. Odd that they pressed so close against the glass door. One cow put her head through the door: she seemed to be holding it open for him. "Mr. Clawsen," the voice was closer now and louder. But the pasture was nearer still, and he hurled himself into it.

"Did he break his neck, Lieutenant?" A patrolman asked Nick, who knelt beside Clawsen.

"No. He's breathing normally. I think he just knocked himself out. Better call an ambulance."

"JAKE SAW IT HIMSELF." Molly showed Margaret his sketch of Clawsen, distraught. "Something he heard during a search committee session completely unhinged him."

"When Jake first showed me this sketchbook," Margaret remembered, "he said even the jovial ones looked anxious a lot of the time."

"Clawsen looks more than anxious."

"I think it must have been the afternoon Lou Stillman called him a *yeshiva bokker*. That really got to him."

"He looks as if the world were ending. Were you discussing Llewellyn's work? He must have realized how close Llewellyn was coming to the material he plagiarized."

"We were talking about sources. Clawsen was objecting that Dick wasn't scholarly enough, hadn't read one thing and another. I brought up the WPA interviews myself." She stopped short. "Oh, God, Molly."

"No. You didn't kill him. Clawsen did." Margaret was still fragile. Molly had not yet suggested a recuperative trip, but she'd already booked the ticket.

"I can't believe he killed them both. He's such a pathetic little drip."

"You don't have to be wonderful to cause a lot of anguish."

"I guess not. But how did he know Jake had seen the interviews too?"

"Nick thinks it was a complete fluke. When his brother died, Clawsen did one of the few decent things he's done recently and flew out to the funeral. The synagogue where the service was held is very close to the Detroit Public Library. Clawsen must have seen Jake, a midcareer fellow from the UAW who, he knew, was taking a labor history course, going into the building, quite possibly to read and reintroduce, so to speak, to Marvell, the documents he'd copied. He made some inquiries, found out Jake had requested and gotten the interviews . . . you know the rest."

"No justice, huh?"

"None we don't make ourselves," Molly said.

THE MAIL HAD COME when Audrey Clawsen got back from the hospital. She took it with her into the kitchen and put the kettle on. While she waited for the water to boil, she sat down with the Talbots catalogue. Although she never ordered anything from them, they sent her the new one every season. She found the perfect suit for Norman's trial on page fifteen; it came in black, cerise, jade, peacock and natural. Black seemed an admission of guilt. Natural, she knew, would show the dirt. Cerise was pretty, and Mrs. Reagan had worn red all the time at daytime functions, but Audrey had been brought up to believe that married women wore red only as an accent. So it came down to jade or peacock. Jade was nice, though perhaps a little harsh and, she feared, unflattering to her complexion. Peacock, on the other hand, brought out the color of her eyes.

Audrey finished her tea and drew a bath. She bathed pensively, then dressed with mounting excitement and purpose. "My husband has been unjustly accused," she would say to the saleslady. "He needs me by his side."